FAERIE WINTER

ALSO BY JANNI LEE SIMNER

Bones of Faerie
Thief Eyes

~ FAERIE WINTER ~

Janni Lee Simner

RANDOM HOUSE NEW YORK

Text copyright © 2011 by Janni Lee Simner
Jacket art copyright © 2011 by Random House, Inc.
Jacket photograph © Fuse/Royalty-Free Jupiter Images
Jacket design by Ellice M. Lee

Visit us on the Web! www.randomhouse.com/teens
Educators and librarians, for a variety of teaching tools,
visit us at www.randomhouse.com/teachers

Library of Congress Cataloging-in-Publication Data
Simner, Janni Lee.
Faerie winter / Janni Lee Simner. — 1st ed.
p. cm.
Summary: Unable to get answers from her mother, sixteen-year-old Liza learns from Karin that while her own actions may have doomed the fairy and human worlds, she may be able to save them with more training, if the Faerie Queen can first be stopped.
ISBN 978-0-375-86671-5 (trade) — ISBN 978-0-375-96671-2 (lib. bdg.) — ISBN 978-0-375-89683-5 (ebook)
[1. Fairies—Fiction. 2. Magic—Fiction. 3. Mothers and daughters—Fiction. 4. Coming of age—Fiction.] I. Title.
PZ7.S594Fae 2011
[Fic]—dc22
2010014250

Printed in the United States of America
10 9 8 7 6 5 4 3 2 1
First Edition

For my nephews, A to Z:

Asher Theodore, Jacob Samuel, and Zachary Elia

Faerie Winter

AUTUMN

The woman who would become my mother backed trembling away from the man who would save her life, and I did not know why. Around them, faerie trees held their bright leaves perfectly still, as if knowing, like I knew, that they saw something they shouldn't.

"How long, Kaylen?" Mom clutched a blanket around her, woven of green rushes. "How long has this magic—"

"I'll hold you no longer." Kaylen, whom I knew as Caleb, looked no younger in this vision than when I'd left for the well this morning. His rumpled linen tunic was green as well, and white flowers were woven into his faerie-clear hair. His bright silver eyes watched Mom with concern but held none of the guarded caution I'd later see there. "I return all your choices back to you."

"How could you hold me at all?" There were flowers in Mom's tangled brown hair, too, dying blooms that fell to the forest floor. In my time she looked older than Caleb, but in this vision she seemed the same age as me.

Caleb dropped to his knees before her. "I was wrong. I see that now, and I beg your forgiveness." He bowed his head. "I put your life before my own until I earn it."

"More oaths. More bindings." Mom's voice cracked. One hand holding the blanket, she grabbed up clothing with the other—denim pants and cotton shirt, human clothes from Before. "I thought it was real, Kaylen. Everything I felt—" She whirled from him and fled into the trees.

"Liza?" A girl's voice, from outside the vision, seeking to draw me back to my own time, my own place. I fought the voice's pull, straining to see where my mother had gone. Instead I saw another woman, walking through the forest.

"That was foolish, Brother," the woman—Karin—said. Her wrists and neck were encircled by green vines, and her brown dress was shot through with streaks of silver, like a child's finger painting. I'd met her when I'd met Caleb.

"Can I do nothing without your spying, Eldest Sister?" Caleb stood to meet her gaze.

The angles of Karin's face were harsher than I remembered. "Perhaps if I had begun spying sooner, you would not be in this tangle. You cannot simply allow your human captive to return to her world, free to speak of her time here as she will. Neither can you keep her in this world, dangerous as any caged animal, only without any illusions to soothe her."

"I have vowed not to bind her. You know as well as I that I must hold to that." A petal fell from Caleb's hair.

Karin caught it and frowned, as if unhappy with the story it told. "Allow me to do it, then. I am not so reckless with my promises as you."

"No."

"She is only human, Kaylen. You do her no harm, any more than hood and jesses do harm to a hawk."

"So I thought once, too." *Caleb stalked past her, in the direction my mother had gone.*

Karin let the petal slip from her fingers. "What do you intend to do, then?"

"This is my responsibility, as you've reminded me often enough." Caleb didn't look back as he walked on. "I will mend it."

"Liza!"

The vision broke up, like fog in the morning sun. I found myself crouched beside the town well and the bucket I'd drawn from it. I looked up, at a girl with an unruly red braid. Allie, who in my time was Caleb's student, put her hands on her hips. "I've been looking and *looking* for you. Don't you even want to say goodbye?"

"Sorry, Allie." I'd gone to the well before dawn, hoping to avoid sun on water and the visions it brought, only to have the moon's light catch me instead. I pressed my palms against my eyes, trying to forget the fear I'd seen on my mother's face. Whatever had happened in my vision, it was past. Mom was safe now.

"Are you all right, Liza?" Allie's face scrunched up as I drew my hands away. "I'm your healer. If anything's wrong, you *have* to tell me."

"It's nothing. Truly." I stood and gave her braid a tug. The sun was just below the horizon, and the autumn leaves around us burned with color. Until a few days ago, I'd never known leaves to change color like this, even when the winter snows began to fall. Ever since the War—since before I was born—the trees had held their green leaves close in all seasons. I still wasn't sure I believed that soon the leaves would drop from those trees, leaving their branches bare.

Allie sighed. "I'm going to miss you so much. You know that, don't you?"

My arms strained as I lifted the bucket. "I'll miss you, too." I'd been as surprised as Allie to learn that she and Caleb were returning to their town, while Mom was staying in mine. Mom and Caleb had cared for each other Before, in Faerie. They'd continued caring through all their years apart, long past when Mom and Father met and I was born, each of them thinking the other had surely perished in the War between their worlds. When Mom had returned to Faerie at last and been poisoned by the War-tainted air there, Caleb had risked his own life to heal her. Yet yesterday Caleb had said he wasn't willing to leave his students to stay with Mom, and Mom had said she wasn't willing to leave hers to stay with him. I glanced uneasily into the bucket, wondering, for the first time, what they both hadn't said.

The first rays of sunlight reflected off the water, but neither Caleb nor Mom appeared in its bright surface. Instead I saw Karin, staring in the direction her brother had gone.

"The Lady will not like this," she said softly. "And this time, Youngest Brother, I do not know how to protect you."

WINTER

⌁ *Chapter 1* ⌁

Snow crunched beneath my boots as I patrolled the winter forest, a gray wolf by my side.

Low on the horizon, a waxing moon shone through the trees, silvering the bare branches of oak and ash, sycamore and elm. Cold bit through the tips of my leather gloves, and my breath puffed into the still air. An oak branch swung at me, sleepy and slow. The wolf—Matthew—growled a warning, but I ducked out of the way easily enough. The oak sighed, but it didn't try again. The trees were too tired to do much harm this winter.

I walked carefully over a line of fire ants melting a trail through the snow. Nearby I heard the clicking of termites chewing dead wood. Termites were among the few creatures who hadn't gone hungry since the leaves had fallen from the trees.

Beneath a pine that had dropped all its needles, a patch of ice-frosted ferns shivered. Something dark moved among the ferns—Matthew's ears stiffened into alertness. I slowed my steps and rested my hand against his back. We walked forward together.

A shadow hunkered amid the ferns, shapeless and trembling. As I knelt before it, the shadow took on a human shape, arms and legs and face, features smudged and indistinct in the moonlight. A child. In one hand it held out a toy, shaped like a dinosaur from Before—long Before.

I removed my glove and took the child's other hand in my own. Shadow fingers passed right through mine, and cold shivered through me. I reached out with my magic, and that magic was cold, too. Cold bound us one to another, shadow and living, strong as twisted rope. Softly I asked, "What is your name?"

Something deep within the shadow yearned toward me, aching to be called back to life. "Ben." His hoarse voice was at the edge of hearing.

I couldn't call any shadow back to life. *"Seek sleep, Ben."* I put my magic—my power—into the words. *"Seek rest, seek darkness, seek peace."*

Icy numbness spread through my fingers. Ben whimpered as he sank into the ferns and the snow. His fingers slipped from mine. "Ethan," he whispered, and then he was gone, leaving behind only a moon-bright whiteness that stung my eyes.

Cold shot through my palm and up my arm. Matthew nudged my other hand, and I remembered the glove I held. I pulled it on. Tingling warmth spread through my fingers, until I could move them once more. "Thanks, Matthew." I pressed my nose to his. Our frosted breaths, human and wolf, mingled in the air.

Matthew made a quiet sound. "Time to go home," I agreed. We turned from the ferns, back toward the path and the chores that waited in town. I scanned the snow and brush around us, but I didn't see any more shadows.

At least it was only human shadows we needed to watch for now. Until this winter, the trees had held shadows of their own, and those shadows had attacked anyone desperate enough to venture out at night. The trees' roots and branches had attacked, too, by day and night both.

But now the trees had dropped their leaves and they slept, and instead human shadows from Before roamed the woods at night, shadows of those who'd died during the War with Faerie. Sometimes those shadows drifted into town, looking for lost loved ones. I still remembered the look on Matthew's grandmother's face when the daughter I hadn't known she'd had appeared at her door. At least she'd let me lay that shadow to rest. Another of our townsfolk had shivered to death when he wouldn't let go of the shadow of his first wife, whom he'd lost during the War. After that, Matthew and I had started doing regular patrols, heading out before dawn a couple of times a week.

We could head out before dawn now that the trees no longer sought human flesh and blood. It had been a welcome change not to fear every rustling leaf.

Matthew stopped and sniffed the air. He turned and trotted off the path, deeper into the forest. I followed. My hand moved to the belt cinched around my oversized coat and the knife that hung sheathed there, a habit from years spent tracking game through more wakeful forests.

Matthew stopped by a mound about the same size he was. He nosed at it, let out a low whine, and began digging. The old snow was unevenly packed, as if it had been shaped by human hands. A faded brown dinosaur sat perched atop it, molded of hard pre-War plastic.

Cold got down beneath my coat and scarf, chilled my toes in their wool socks. I helped Matthew dig, knowing well enough what we would find.

Ben had been young, little more than a toddler, with curls that hung frozen over a face made pale by the moonlight. He hadn't died in the War after all. He'd died no more than a day or two ago, after the last snowfall, and someone had buried him here.

I wanted nothing more to do with dead children. I wanted to flee this place, but we had to know what had happened to him, in case it posed some danger to our town.

Cold stiffened my fingers. The dinosaur toppled into the snow. I kept digging.

∽ *Chapter 2* ∼

Whoever had buried Ben had closed his eyes before covering him. Last night's wind had left no tracks, no sign of where that someone might have gone. The nearest towns were all at least a day's walk away from ours. What had this child been doing here, so far from home?

As Matthew and I dug the snow away, Ben's cold hand emerged, clenched against his chest as if he still held his toy. His sweater was a mess of charred fibers that crumbled at my touch. Beneath them—I fought not to look away.

Matthew whined. Beneath Ben's sweater, the flesh was melted, wool fused to blackened skin and frozen blisters. I was glad of the cold, which kept the odor at bay. I was glad I'd not yet eaten. Matthew's ears drooped, and I put my arms around him, squeezing hard, breathing the frosty smell of his fur. If there'd been a fire nearby, he should have caught some scent of it. How far had Ben fled after he'd been burned, and why?

I laid him to rest. There was nothing more we could do. I piled snow over Ben once more. Matthew took the toy dinosaur in his teeth and placed it carefully atop the grave. We headed for home as the moon slipped below the horizon and a faint band of gray lit the eastern sky.

In the distance, an owl hooted sleepily. An owl's talons could tear a person open easily enough—but when I heard the sound again, it was farther off. The deer and rabbits and mice were going hungry with the trees asleep, and that meant the owls and hawks and wild dogs were hungry, too. When they attacked, they were harder to scare off, but there'd been fewer of them as winter had worn on. We'd have been suffering more from the lack of game in town, too, if not for the emergency provisions we'd been able to lay in the past few years.

Pale yellow light smudged the horizon by the time Matthew and I reached the fields outside our town, Franklin Falls. A brown ragweed vine swung sleepily back and forth across our path. I cut the thing free and flung it into the forest. It could do little harm now, but when spring came, such vines would once again seek our blood.

If spring came. My gaze strayed to the fields beside

the path. They were white with new snow, only a few dead grasses poking through. The shivering green leaves of winter potatoes and turnips and beets should have long since broken the frozen soil, but this year they hadn't grown at all. My hand moved to Matthew's back, and he edged closer to me. We relied on those root vegetables to help us through the spring while we waited for corn and beans and squash to grow.

The adults said that these dead fields had been normal Before, that there'd been no winter crops and spring had always come just the same. Yet even they'd grown uneasy when the pines and firs had gone brown and dropped their needles. Why trees dropping needles should be more unsettling than trees dropping leaves, I didn't know, but after that, the Council agreed that we should go on short rations until the spring crops came in—just to be safe, they said.

"What if it's all my fault?" I asked Matthew as my boots and his paws left prints in the snow behind us. Last week patches of brown earth had shown through, but two days ago new snow had covered them again.

Matthew gave my knee a sharp nudge. We'd had this discussion before: Matthew insisted that I wasn't to blame, that there was no way I could have known what would happen, and that spring would likely still come.

I thought of a hillside thick with blackberry and

sumac, all dead now; of the cinnamon-barked quia tree that stood among the brambles. I'd called that faerie tree into the human world, though only a few people knew it. Magic flowed in two directions; the same power that allowed me to command shadows to rest allowed me to command—to *call*—seeds to grow. But the quia seed had come from a dead land beyond both my world and Faerie, and now I feared I'd called death into my world as well.

I hadn't thought so at first. I'd laughed with the others to see the leaves burst into fiery colors and fall from the trees, and thought only of how much easier winter would be if the trees slept and we could walk through the forest unafraid. That had been nearly a half year ago, though. The leaves had since turned to brown, and the world their falling had left behind reminded me of the black-and-white photos in the oldest books from Before. It reminded me of the land where I'd found the quia seed. I hadn't known that any world could be so gray.

I'd tried calling the winter crops as I'd called the seed. They hadn't listened. I'd tried to call acorns and maple seeds, remembering how I'd once sensed the green at the heart of all seeds yearning to grow. I'd felt nothing but a shadowy gray silence. I'd had no better luck calling leaves from the bare branches of the quia tree itself. The days were as long as the nights now, and winter still hadn't released its hold on the land. I could fight a willow's strangling roots, or a hawk's poisoned talons, but I didn't know how to fight a world that didn't want to grow.

We left the fields behind, walking past the ruins of splintered houses half-buried in tangles of dead ragweed and wild grape. At the edge of the ruins, a once-abandoned house awaited painting. Beyond it we came to the row of whitewashed homes that was our town. As Matthew and I followed the path alongside them, I saw Jayce—the town blacksmith—walking toward us, limping from his old hunting injury. As he waved, I pulled my fur hat more firmly down over my ears and made sure my hair was tucked into my collar. My magic was no longer a secret—nor was anyone else's—but the clear streaks in my hair were more reminder of it than most folks were comfortable with.

"Liza." Jayce's hand gripped his cane, his skin scarred from years spent working in the forge. His gaze flicked to the wolf at my side. "Matthew." Matthew's walking through town as a wolf was more reminder of magic than many were comfortable with, too, but Matthew didn't try to hide, not since the meeting at which we'd told the town that all its children either had magic or one day would. That meeting had gone better than I'd feared: only two adults had drawn their knives, and while one of the children had caused earth tremors with his magic, he'd stopped them before it became clear he was the cause. Until then, our town had cast out all magic for fear of the harm it could do—of the harm it had done, during the War. Once the townsfolk learned that every child born after the War was touched by magic, however, they had little choice. They couldn't cast us *all* out, though there were those who wanted to try. Jayce wasn't one of them. He'd had enough of dead children, too.

"Find anything out there?" The blacksmith's gaze remained on me, not Matthew.

"A boy." I rubbed Matthew's ears. "Young, no more than three."

"And you took care of him?"

I stared at the condensation frozen in Jayce's bushy beard and brows. "Not just a shadow. We found a body as well." I told him all that we'd seen. Sun lit the thin streaks of high clouds. If the cold didn't break, in a day or two there'd be more snow.

The blacksmith ran a hand over his bald head, which bore more scars. "Council meets tonight. I'll tell them. If there's time, maybe we can send someone to bury him— only once the snow melts, we'll all need to be out planting." If he feared that the spring crops wouldn't grow, he gave no sign. Adults believed, somewhere deep inside, that spring would come, for all that they were careful of our rations. Some part of them couldn't imagine that green wouldn't return to the world, as if green was something we were born to. I did not understand it. Deep inside *I* felt as if this gray had surely gone on forever and the forests I'd fought all my life had been merely illusions.

Jayce blew a puff of frost into the air. "It can't be an easy thing, walking with ghosts. You're a good girl, Liza. I always told your father so. I think he'd be proud of you, if only . . ." He shook his head. Surely he knew that Father wouldn't be proud of me if he saw me using my magic so openly, no matter that I used it to protect my town. Father would have killed me for that magic if he could have, just as he'd killed my baby sister, even though I was too old simply to be left out on a hillside to die. He'd have drawn his knife across my throat, only I'd used my magic to send him away instead.

"Take care Liza, all right?" Jayce hesitated, then looked at the wolf. "You too, Matthew." He continued down the path toward his forge, and Matthew and I continued to my house.

I heard voices out back. We walked around to find Mom and Hope crouched in the snow.

"Gently," Mom said. "A breath of wind, nothing more."

Hope closed her eyes and held out her bare hands. A breeze rippled over the snow, catching the thin blond braids that fringed her face. Tiny acorns clattered at the braids' ends. A foolish risk, some said. I knew I wasn't willing to trust an acorn enough to wear it so close to my face, winter or no winter. But ever since Hope and her new husband had moved into their own home, she seemed to have given up on caring what others thought.

The white snow in front of her drifted upward. Hope grinned, a mischievous look that made it hard to believe she was older than Matthew and me. At nearly eighteen she was the oldest person in our town with magic.

"Control," Mom whispered. I tried not to focus on how loosely her down-filled coat hung about her shoulders, or the way the shadows around her eyes gave her face a sunken look that hadn't been there last summer.

Hope's breeze gusted, blowing cold white powder into all of our faces. I coughed; Matthew shook snow from his fur. Hope laughed, brushed the snow from her jacket, and got to her feet. "This is gonna be hell once the baby starts kicking." Her hands moved to her belly, though there was little sign yet that she was pregnant.

Mom smiled. Did anyone else see the tiredness behind it? "That's why you need to work on control now. Practice whenever you can."

"Yes, ma'am," Hope said, but there was no serious-ness in it. She ruffled Matthew's fur. "You two getting into any trouble?"

Matthew barked. My face flushed.

"And why not?" Hope pulled on her gloves.

Before I could answer, Matthew shrugged his wolf's shoulders. Hope laughed again. "See you all later. I'll practice, Tara, I promise." She gave Mom a quick hug and headed home with a final wave.

Mom hugged me, too, more tightly, as if determined to keep me close. I hugged her back, feeling her bony shoulder blades through her coat. She headed inside, and Matthew and I followed, through the back door and into the cold kitchen, where Matthew's clothes lay scat-tered on the floor. He hung behind as Mom and I con-tinued into the living room.

Mom had built up the fire. I pulled off my gloves and warmed my chilled hands over the coals. I loosened my scarf, unbuttoned my coat, and shoved my hat and gloves into my pockets. The coat had no lack of pockets; it was Father's old army jacket from Before. Wearing his coat felt strange, but I'd outgrown mine, and I welcomed the warmth of the bear-fur lining he'd added.

Mom shrugged off her coat and pulled off her gloves, too. Without thinking, I searched for the silver leaf she'd worn all her life, a gift from Caleb—but she'd removed it the day Caleb had left our town, and I hadn't seen it since. I'd not told either of them about the vision I'd had that day. I thought of Mom, trembling as she'd fled from Caleb—but she hadn't seemed frightened when she'd taken off the leaf, only sad.

I watched as Mom took a pot holder and removed the teapot from the rack above the fire. She poured hot tea into a mug and pressed the warm mug into my hands with a little too much force, as if that, too, were a way of holding me close.

Heat spread through my chest as I drank. My stomach grumbled, but I ignored it. If I could wait until after my morning chores to eat, I'd be less hungry the rest of the day.

Mom put her hands over mine. Her fingers were too thin, bone pressing against skin. "You're cold, Lizzy. More trouble? You didn't have any nightmares last night, so I slept right through your leaving."

I inhaled the mint-scented steam. "Nothing I couldn't handle."

Mom gave me a searching look. "What happened?"

I looked at the mug as I repeated all I'd told Jayce. SeaWorld San Diego, it read. I wondered, not for the first time, where San Diego was, and whether it had survived the War, and how you made a world of the sea.

Mom ran a hand through her lank hair. "I wish you didn't have to go out there."

"I do what needs doing." No one else's magic could lay ghosts to rest.

"We both do." Matthew's human footsteps crossed the room.

I turned and saw that his frown reached to his serious gray eyes—he didn't like Mom's complaining about our patrols, either. I longed to run a finger along his down-turned lips, but I didn't.

Mom sighed. "I just wish I could keep you safe." She filled a mug for Matthew, too, one with a picture of a thorny green plant that looked as if it shouldn't have existed before the War. Arizona-Sonora Desert Museum, the mug read.

The tea burned my throat as I finished it. *You never kept me safe.*

Matthew drank his tea in a few quick gulps. "Thanks, Tara," he told Mom. His fingers brushed mine, and the light touch tingled over my skin. Matthew and I kept each other safe. He was the one person in this town I trusted beyond all doubting.

"See you later, Liza?" A few strands had escaped his blond ponytail. I resisted the urge to brush the hair back from his face, even as I imagined drawing him near enough for our lips to touch as gently as our fingers had. As always, the thought made me feel strangely shy. What if Matthew could read it in my face, as clearly as I could read the angle of his wolf's ears, the tenor of his bark? What if I acted on it, only to find he didn't feel the same way?

"Later," I agreed. I stared at the way his shoulders stretched the fabric of his sweater and at the downy fuzz on his chin and cheeks, which had nothing to do with his shifting and which hadn't been there when winter began. I'd buried my face against his fur often enough. Why did I hesitate so much more when he was human than when he was a wolf? I watched as he grabbed his coat from the couch and headed out to help his grandmother with their morning chores.

Mom put her hand on my shoulder as the door shut behind him. "I thought we could practice control this morning, too. You've gotten so good with your calling this winter. Now we just have to work on applying that to your visions."

I wasn't sure my visions could be controlled. The harder I tried, the more they caught me unaware. Sometimes I wasn't even sure whether it was the past or the future I saw.

And where were you, Mom, when I started having visions? For more than two years, all the children in my town had known they could go to Mom and Matthew's grandmother with their magic—except for me.

Mom had no magic of her own. No human born before the War had magic; all those born After did. But Mom had spent time in Faerie Before—time with Caleb—and knew more about magic than most. She'd taught the others as well as she could, in secret so that Father wouldn't find out. Matthew's grandmother had helped her. Matthew and Hope and the others had been Mom's students, and they'd all known about each other's magic, though they'd never spoken of it aloud where those without magic could hear. Mom said she'd feared that Father would kill me if he learned I knew about the magic in our town, so she'd hidden that magic from me. She said she'd been protecting me and the others both. But after Father had abandoned my sister to die, Mom had run away to what remained of Faerie, leaving me alone with him. Sending Father away had fallen to me and my magic after all— the magic Mom hadn't known I had until after she'd left.

My throat felt dry. I picked up my mug and remembered that it was empty. "There's work to do." There was more work now that Father was gone.

"I already brought in the water," Mom said.

"Mom!" My fingers tightened around the mug's handle.

"I'm not an invalid, Liza. You don't have to do everything. I brought in the eggs, too. It's not our turn with the sheep or goats, so we're okay there."

I looked at Mom's thin shoulders. "Caleb told you not to push too hard."

"Kaylen doesn't know everything." Mom used his faerie name from Before, as she often did. She took the mug from me. "I left you the firewood, if you really feel you haven't worked hard enough today." Mom set my mug on the shelf above the fireplace, beside other chipped mugs from Before. She reached for Matthew's mug as well, then stopped short and clutched her stomach.

"What's wrong?" I grabbed her as she stumbled, and helped her over to the couch.

"It's nothing." Mom sighed as she sat down. A hank of wool lay on a drop cloth beside the couch, and she took up a handful of it. "Go get that wood, if you're so eager to escape your lessons." She grabbed the metal-toothed hand carders from the table and began pulling wool through them.

I watched her fingers grow shiny with sheep oil, fighting the fear that had stalked me ever since I'd found Mom and brought her out of Faerie, fear that Caleb hadn't fully healed her after all.

"I'm *fine*, Liza." Mom didn't look up as she continued carding the wool.

I wanted to believe that, but Mom had lied to me before. How was I to know when to trust her? I stalked past her and out the door before I could ask the question aloud.

The clouds were thicker now. I buttoned my coat and pulled on hat and gloves as I walked through the town and down a side path to the Store where we kept our firewood. I could barely make out the words *General Mercantile* above the door. The rest of the sign, proclaiming that the Store sold ice, fudge, and cigarettes, had long since faded away.

The door creaked as I opened it, stepping into a dim room piled high with stacked firewood. Gathering wood had been easier with the trees asleep. Behind the Store's metal counter, I heard whispers.

I found Kyle there, lying on his stomach, talking to a row of black ants with a metallic blue-green sheen. Carpenter ants. Though they made no sound, I knew that the ants spoke to Kyle, too. Kyle was an animal speaker and, at five years old, the youngest surviving child in our town to have come into his magic.

Anyone who could talk to carpenter ants knew they didn't belong in a woodshed. Kyle looked up at me, as furtive as if he'd been caught dipping a finger into the honey. He had a streak of dirt across his nose, and a slick of black hair stuck straight up from his head. "They say the wood is warm. They say they want to stay."

"They can't stay," I told Kyle. His coat and rumpled pants looked like they'd been slept in. Perhaps they had—at the meeting during which we'd told the towns-folk about our magic, Kyle's mother, Brianna, had wanted to force Kyle and his older brother out of the house, only their father wouldn't allow it. It was their father who'd shivered to death holding his first wife's shadow too close less than a month later. As far as I could tell, Kyle's mother could barely stand to look at her children now.

A half dozen ants climbed onto Kyle's fingers, which were losing their baby thickness. If the ants feasted on our firewood—or the Stores' timbers—we'd have a problem. "If they stay, we'll have to lay down poison."

"It's not their fault!" Kyle hunched protectively over the small creatures. "It's cold outside."

It wasn't a hawk's fault it had to eat, either, but that didn't mean I was obligated to let one gut me for its dinner. "There are other warm places. Tell them to find one." Ants, like termites, had the entire sleeping forest to feast on this winter.

Kyle stroked the ant crawling over his thumb, as if it were some tame creature, as if its colony couldn't bring the Store down around our ears.

"They're *ants*, Kyle."

The boy stuck out his lower lip. "Don't be mean."

Could Kyle talk to deer and rabbits, too? How would he hunt when he got older? One way or another, he'd have to learn to care less for the animals he talked with. "The ants will be fine. They're good marchers."

Kyle's face scrunched up, as if he was thinking about that. He cupped his hands, whispered words too low to hear, and set his hands down on the floor.

The ants on his fingers crawled to the ground and began marching toward the door. Other ants followed, from the floor around Kyle, their insect legs moving in perfect unison. More ants emerged from the woodpiles— so many. Kyle hummed an old work song from Before under his breath. *The ants go marching one by one . . .*

I smiled at that. "Where'd you send them?"

Kyle flashed me a grin as he scrambled to his feet. "Into Johnny's pants."

"Kyle!" Johnny was Kyle's older brother. I tried to sound severe, but if there was anyone whose pants I'd not mind seeing crawl with ants, it was Johnny.

"Ants in pants." Kyle laughed as if he'd done the funniest thing imaginable. "They promised not to bite."

Did ants keep their promises? I doubted they could even find Kyle's brother, given how hard Johnny's stalking magic made it for anyone to find him lately.

"Don't stay too long," I told Kyle as I headed for one of the woodpiles. "Your mom'll be looking for you."

Kyle's laughter died. "No. She won't." He looked down at his boots.

I piled wood into my arms. At least Brianna was feeding Kyle and, as far as I could tell, not lifting her hands to him. Still, I glanced back uneasily as I stepped over the ants and out the door. Kyle's focus was back on the insects; he didn't seem to see me leave.

Outside, the wind blew harder, carrying a faint burned-leather smell. From the forest beyond the Store, I heard a foot break the snow, a ragged breath caught and held. I set the wood down and turned.

As I did, a stranger fled deeper into the forest.

~ *Chapter 3* ~

I ran after the stranger, a boy around my age. Snow flew up from our boots as we wove among the bare trees. Patches of his burned sweater fell into the snow behind him. Had he been caught in the same fire as Ben? Was he the one who'd buried the younger boy?

The distance between us grew. *"Stop!"* I put my magic into the command. I'd been too late to save Ben, but I might not be too late for this boy. Remembering Ben's final word, I called, *"Ethan, come here!"*

The boy skidded to a halt in a small clearing, snow flying in his wake, and I knew the name was his. He turned and walked back toward me, steps as stiff as those of Kyle's ants, eyes as wild as those of a deer trapped in a hawthorn thicket. His hands were shoved into the charred pockets of his pants and his tangled curls reminded me of Ben.

"Is your town safe?" the boy asked.

"Safe from what?" No town was wholly safe from fire—but the fire didn't explain why Ben had fled after he'd been burned. I narrowed my eyes. "What happened in your town?"

"It wasn't my fault. The children—I tried—" Ethan's legs trembled, and he crumpled into the snow. Beside him a redbud shivered its irritation, sighed, and was still.

"What wasn't your fault?" I crouched beside him. Whatever danger his town had faced, my town needed to know about it.

Tentative footsteps came up behind me. Kyle reached out to touch the boy's face. "Hot."

I put a hand to Ethan's forehead. His skin burned with fever. "Get your mom," I told Kyle. As the town's midwife, Brianna was the nearest thing we had to a doctor.

Kyle shook his head. "Not Mom." He pointed to Ethan's pockets. Wisps of smoke rose from them. The burned-leather smell in the air grew stronger.

"Mom doesn't do magic." Kyle looked up at me, as if expecting some answer to that.

"Get Kate, then." Matthew's grandmother knew some things about healing, too. "No—get Matthew." Matthew could help carry Ethan to their house.

Kyle nodded and ran into town, arms flapping at his sides. I reached to draw Ethan's hands from his pockets, but he moaned and pulled himself into a tight ball. The smoke stopped.

A few minutes later Matthew came running through the snow, Kyle at his heels. Matthew glanced at Ethan, gave my gloved hand a quick squeeze—his fingers were bare, as if he'd left in a hurry—and turned to Kyle. "Another firestarter?"

Kyle bit his lip. "Is this one going to die, too?"

Matthew rubbed at the ragged scar around his wrist. "I don't know." The look that passed between him and Kyle was filled with the years they'd secretly learned about magic from Mom while I'd thought my town free of magic. Just as I'd thought Jayce's granddaughter had died of a fever, and not from trying so hard to control her fire magic that it had burned her from within.

"Council meeting's at my house tonight," Matthew said. "We have to take him to your place, Liza. Gram will join us there."

I doubted we could keep this stranger secret from the Council for long, even if we wanted to, but there was no sense asking for trouble. I helped Matthew lift Ethan into a fireman's carry over his shoulders. Ethan whimpered as his hands fell free. They were covered with weeping blisters. Had his firestarting slipped beyond his control, and was that how Ben had died? Would it be safer to leave Ethan in the forest after all?

I kept the thought to myself. I was done casting magic out if I could help it. I followed Matthew and Ethan to my house, picking up the firewood along the way. Kyle trailed behind me.

Mom and Kate met us at the door and urged us all inside. I set the wood by the fire and helped Matthew settle Ethan on the couch. Mom brushed the tangles back from the stranger's face. I saw no sign of the pain that had made her bend over earlier.

Matthew's grandmother, Kate, knelt by the boy's side, her hair pulled back in its usual efficient gray bun. Once her knees wouldn't have let her kneel, but Allie had healed them before she and Caleb left us. Kate frowned as she put her soft weaver's hands to the boy's forehead. "We need to bring his fever down. Matthew, get him upstairs into the tub. Liza, start filling buckets. Use water—snow's too cold."

Kyle tugged on my sleeve as I headed for the door. "I can help."

"Buckets are too heavy for you." Surely Kyle knew that, just as he knew ants couldn't be allowed in the woodpiles.

Kyle stuck out his lower lip. "I *can*."

Kate and Mom exchanged looks. "Let him go with you," Kate said softly. "He'll have to go home soon enough."

I sighed, but I didn't stop Kyle as he followed me out the door. I grabbed a wooden bucket from around back and carried it toward the well. Kyle dragged a second bucket through the snow behind him.

Another boy from our town, Seth, was there drawing water, one hand extended over the well shaft, the other absently turning the crank. At seventeen Seth was a year older than Matthew and me, with close-cut hair and a lazy look that made him seem half-asleep. The bucket moved toward him, but the rope was too slack for his cranking to be lifting it; he must have been using his object calling. He tensed at the sound of Kyle's and my footsteps, as if the habit of hiding magic hadn't wholly left him, but he kept using his magic to float the bucket out of the well. "Hi, Liza. Kyle. What's going on?" He unhooked the bucket and it drifted to the ground beside him.

Kyle let go of his bucket and said, "Liza found a firestarter."

How had Mom and Kate ever kept magic a secret with Kyle around? I hooked my bucket onto the rope and lowered it. "A boy," I told Seth. "Found him just outside of town. Water's to get his fever down." Liquid sloshed into my bucket. As I started cranking it up again, I watched Seth's half-lidded eyes, gauging his reaction. Like me, Seth had once helped turn strangers away from our town.

"Firestarting. That's rough." Seth reached out a hand, and the tension left the crank. My bucket rose out of the well to hover in front of me. I nodded my thanks as I unhooked it. The bucket drifted gently to the ground.

Kyle grabbed his bucket and held it out to me. I sighed, took it, and lowered it into the well. I lifted the full bucket out—Seth helped again—and set it down in front of Kyle. He'd see soon enough that he couldn't carry it.

Kyle pressed his lips together, looking determined, and reached for the bucket with both hands.

It came up easily in his hold. Kyle grinned. So did Seth, who had his arm stretched toward it.

I rolled my eyes. "He'll never learn that way."

Seth shrugged. "Why make things harder than they have to be?" He hefted his own bucket without magic. "Come on. Show me this firestarter. Chores can wait—I'll haul what I can. We Afters have to stick together."

Afters. Those born since the War. Seth and Kyle followed me back to my house. Outside, we met Matthew, who was frowning as he carried another bucket toward the well. I went inside ahead of Kyle and Seth. Kyle insisted on "carrying" his bucket all the way up the stairs behind me.

Like all the upstairs rooms, the bathroom was cold, because houses built Before had fireplaces only on their lowest floors. Ethan lay naked and shivering in the claw-foot tub, his eyes squeezed shut. Mom rubbed his forehead with a damp cloth while Kate wrapped bandages around his blistered hands. The rest of Ethan's body wasn't burned, not even his chest, in spite of his charred sweater. That made little sense. Did magic somehow protect firestarters from their own fires?

I was staring. I looked away, resting my bucket beside the tub, while Seth and Kyle waited in the hallway. Kate finished wrapping his hands and nodded at me. I began pouring the water in.

Ethan screamed at the touch of cold water on his fevered skin. I drew the bucket back. He jerked upright, huddling over and glaring at us all through wild eyes.

The bandage on his left hand had come loose. Kate tightened it and gently took both his hands in hers. "Keep going, Liza."

I poured the water more slowly this time. Ethan rocked back and forth, shivering still. "Not my fault," he whimpered. "Not my fault."

No one said anything wasn't their fault unless they feared it was. I took the empty bucket into the hall. Kyle walked past me, head held high, hands barely touching his own bucket as it floated in front of him. Seth followed close behind him.

With three of us working—four, counting Kyle—it

only took a few trips to fill the tub. Somewhere in the cabinets Kyle found a trio of faded green rubber frogs and balanced them on the tub's edge. Ethan didn't seem to notice. He stopped whimpering and stared, wide-eyed, at the ceiling.

"It's all right," Mom whispered to him, over and over again, just like she had when I was small.

Like me, this stranger knew better. "Not all right. Never all right."

I thought of Ben's burned body. "What happened?" I asked him. Mom gave me a sharp look. "We have to know," I said.

"Time enough for that later." Kate still held Ethan's hands, keeping them out of the water. "Fever's already down a little," she said.

Ethan moaned. Mom made shushing sounds. "You're safe here."

The boy frowned, as if safety were a child's tale he'd long ago stopped believing.

Once we got Ethan into bed, he fell into a fitful sleep. Mom kept watch over him while Matthew, Seth, and I headed off to other chores. Kyle followed me into the forest to gather acorns hidden beneath the snow. I let him. Gathering was a task a child could help with, now that the trees slept. In years past the oaks had held their acorns close or else flung them at passersby in hopes they'd root in skin and bone, but this autumn they'd fallen like rain from the trees—not only small acorns, such as those Hope wore, but larger ones as well. Soaked, acorn kernels made a bitter flour, one that had gotten us through a couple of hard years when I was small. *Famine food,* Kate called it. I didn't look forward to eating such again, but if the spring crops didn't come in, the acorns would give us a little more time, until they ran out as well.

Kyle really did help with the gathering, at least until he found a glowworm melting a trail through the snow and stopped to talk to it.

"Don't touch it," I warned him. Usually glowworms didn't hold much heat, but with so much leaf litter for them to feed on this winter, they were burning hotter than usual.

Kyle gave me a long look, as though he couldn't believe I'd think him so stupid, and turned back to the worm, leaving me to finish filling the acorn sack myself. When I was done, the worm was gone, but Kyle's name was spelled out in worm trails in the snow. My stomach ached with hunger by then, and I wished I'd eaten before heading out after all.

As we returned to town, Kyle's mother marched over

to us and grabbed his arm. "What trouble are you making *now*?" Brianna demanded.

Kyle stared at the ground. I pointed to the acorn sack. "He wasn't any trouble. He was a good helper."

Kyle's mother gave me a smoldering look. "You'll do well not to tell me when my son is and isn't making trouble, Liza." She dragged Kyle away. He didn't protest, just kept looking down with a sullen frown as his mother began muttering about what a useless child he was. I winced, though they were only words. I knew well enough that words could cut deep as blows.

I brought the sack home and set it down on the couch along with my scarf, hat, and gloves. Before this winter, I wouldn't have dared bring acorns within walls until they were soaked and ground into meal, but I felt no more life in these seeds than I'd felt in the others.

The morning's fire had burned down to hot coals. I unbuttoned my coat but kept it on as I set yesterday's cornmeal mush over the heat. There was some squirrel left in the mush, and my stomach grumbled as it simmered. I took the pot from the fire, filled two bowls, and brought them upstairs along with a couple of spoons.

Father's—no, *Mom's*—door was open. I stepped into the chilly room. Ethan slept on the feather bed, more easily now, his bandaged hands resting loosely atop the covers. Mom sat in a chair beside him, darning holes in old socks. I handed her a bowl. From the dresser, a small oil lamp added its light to the sun shining in around the nylon-tacked windows.

"Lunchtime already?" Mom set the mending aside and took the bowl absently into her lap. She tilted her head toward Ethan. "Kate gave him something to help him sleep."

I put a spoon into Mom's bowl and sat beside her in the room's other chair. Mom sighed and swallowed a mouthful. Once she ate, I did, too. My stomach's grumbling eased.

Too soon, Mom stopped and handed me her bowl. "You finish it, Liza."

I shook my head, though my bowl was empty and I could easily have scraped Mom's clean as well. "I'll save it for later." Mom was eating too little as it was. I took both bowls downstairs and spooned the cornmeal back into the pot. Grabbing the acorn sack and a nutcracker, I headed back upstairs, where Mom was wiping Ethan's face with a wet cloth.

"Do you think he killed Ben?" I asked her.

Mom set the cloth aside. "I think it likely."

My damp socks were cold. "Do you wish I'd left him in the forest?"

"There are those who would do that in this town and not regret it. I know that well enough." Mom looked at

Ethan as she spoke. "I am glad to learn my daughter is not one of them."

Ethan whimpered in his sleep. Wisps of smoke escaped the bandages around his hands. Mom scrambled to her feet and grabbed a water basin from beside the bed. She shoved it into my hands, pulled Ethan up, and plunged his hands into the water, which sizzled at the sudden heat. Ethan cried out and fought Mom, but she didn't release him until the sizzling stopped. Tears streamed down his face as he fell back to the bed. I returned the basin to the floor as Mom moved Ethan's arms back to his sides. Neither of us spoke until he'd settled back into sleep.

Mom sighed as she straightened his blankets. "He has far less control than Jayce's granddaughter did. That worries me. I don't know as much about the wilder magics, like those that deal with fire and plants. If I did, maybe our firestarter would have lived."

I drew an acorn from the bag. Caleb's sister Karin was a plant mage. "Karin's magic isn't wild." She had better control than anyone I knew.

Mom picked up her darning from where it had fallen to the floor. "I still can't imagine Karinna teaching humans."

I opened my mouth, strangely stung. It was Karin who'd first taught me about magic, while Mom had still been keeping her teaching secret from me. "Karin saved my life." When mulberry trees had attacked Matthew and me, she'd rescued us. I thought of how harsh she'd been to Caleb in my vision. That vision didn't match the woman I knew. "Karin was kind to me."

"But not to me," Mom said.

She is only human, Kaylen. You do her no harm, any more than hood and jesses do harm to a hawk. It was Mom Karin had been speaking about. That didn't fit what I knew of her, either. Karin taught an entire town full of human children.

But before that, Karin had fought against my people in the War. Allie had told me so.

I turned the acorn in my hands. I suspected that this was about neither Karin's teaching nor which side she'd fought on. "Karin didn't like you and Caleb being together, did she?" The vision had made that clear enough.

Mom moved her needle through the wool with slow, careful stitches. She never spoke of her time in Faerie, no matter how often I asked. The memory of how frightened she'd been in my vision kept me from asking too often, but it didn't make my questions go away. "Can you at least tell me how the War started?"

Mom pushed her needle too hard; it punched through the wool to stab her finger. She cursed and brought her finger to her lips. "Right. I need a break. You up for taking a turn with Ethan?"

For years I'd thought I knew how the War had begun—the faerie folk had attacked us, for reasons of their own. Now that I'd seen the damage my people had done to Faerie in turn, I knew it couldn't be that simple. "Why won't you tell me?"

Mom stood and looked at me. A drop of blood had beaded on her fingertip. "There's some who'd say Kaylen—Caleb—and I started the War. Last time I spoke to her, Karinna was among them."

She left the room before I could ask anything more.

I shelled acorns while I kept watch over Ethan. Twice more his bandages smoldered, and I doused his hands in the water. The second time the charred bandages crumbled away. I wrapped new ones loosely around his burns. I could have called Mom up to help me, but I didn't. How much longer did I have to fear hurting her with my questions?

How could she and Caleb possibly have caused the War?

The sun grew low as I continued shelling. I heard a soft creak on the stairs. Matthew stepped into the room with another nutcracker. I gave his hand a quick squeeze. His fingers were cold. He sat, and we shelled together.

Matthew looked toward Ethan. "How is he?"

"About the same." I wanted to reach for Matthew's hand again, to warm it between both of mine, but then I wouldn't be able to work.

Matthew picked at a stubborn bit of shell. "Gram's going to tell them about Ethan at the Council meeting tonight. She says it's best they hear it from her."

"Kyle probably already told his mom. She's in a foul mood today. She'll want to send Ethan away."

Matthew tossed the acorn shell into the growing pile beside me. "The Council will likely be split. Gram says it's going to be a long meeting."

I listened to Ethan's steady breathing as I took another acorn from the sack. If we sent him away now, he'd die in the forest and the snow.

Matthew pressed his lips together. "We won't let them make Ethan leave. I already spoke to Hope and Seth. Charlotte, too." Those were all the older Afters. "If this town wants to send him away, they'll have to get past all of us first." He looked at me, and I knew he wanted to know if I'd stand with them. He'd always stood by me, even when I'd done little to deserve it.

I hesitated, then voiced my fear aloud. "What if Ethan really is a danger to our town? We don't even know that Ben's death was an accident. And even if it was, it's an accident that could happen again."

"We'll deal with it." Matthew sounded very sure.

I envied his certainty. "I won't let you stand alone, if it comes down to that." My fingers tightened around the acorn. The Council made the rules for Franklin Falls. What would happen if we challenged them? "It's risky." I was shivering. I just couldn't seem to get warm this winter. Matthew put his arm around my shoulders, and together we watched the rise and fall of Ethan's chest.

"Nothing's safe," Matthew said.

I knew that better than anyone. I turned to him. Strands of blond hair fell around Matthew's face, and his eyes were strangely bright. I shivered harder. Then, since I was already being brave, I leaned forward and brushed my lips against his.

He didn't pull away as I'd feared. With a soft sound he drew me closer, reaching up to run his fingers through my hair. His musky taste reminded me of the smell of his wolf's fur. The acorn in my hand pattered to the floor.

The rustling of blankets made us pull abruptly apart. Ethan sat up in bed, staring at us.

Matthew's ears flushed red. My face burned. I wondered if Ethan could *see* the way the taste of Matthew's lips lingered on mine. The boy's eyes hardened as he focused on us. He didn't trust us.

I didn't fully trust him, either. "How are you feeling?"

"How do you think I feel?" Ethan huddled down among the blankets. "But at least I'm still alive, right? I ought to be grateful." His voice was bitter, as if maybe he wished we hadn't saved him.

Why had he come to our town if he didn't want to be saved? "What are you doing here?" I demanded.

"Looking for someplace safe." There was a challenge in Ethan's words.

I couldn't promise him safety. I didn't try. "Where are you from?"

"Clayburn." Ethan looked down at his hands as if seeing the bandages for the first time. His breathing sped up.

I thought of the maps I'd seen. Clayburn was one of the nearer towns, about a day's walk away. "Was Ben from Clayburn, too?"

Ethan bolted to his feet, blankets falling away, nightshirt barely covering his knees. "How do you know about that?" He backed through the doorway and into the hall.

"*Ethan!*" My voice tightened around the call. I couldn't let him go. I had to know why he was afraid, and whether his magic had truly killed, and, if it had, how likely it was to kill again. "*Ethan, stop!*"

He jerked to a stop, just as I'd commanded. I felt the cold thread of my magic stretching between us.

Fear crept into his eyes. "You did that before, too, didn't you? Just like she did."

"Like who did?" I walked past Ethan, putting myself between him and the stairs. Matthew followed with the water basin.

"Let me go." Smoke rose from Ethan's bandages. "Let me go or I'll *kill* you, I swear it."

"Liza." There was a warning in Matthew's voice.

I ignored it, keeping my gaze and my magic focused on Ethan. "Like you killed Ben?"

Flames burst through Ethan's bandages. The magic binding him to me burned away as charred linen drifted to the floor. The boy drew his hands together, cupping a ball of fire within.

Matthew flung the water at him. The fire hissed but didn't go out. The scent of damp coals filled the air.

Matthew held the basin in front of us like a shield. "Easy, Ethan. We won't hurt you."

"*You* won't, maybe." Ethan's dark eyes reflected the fire he held. I felt its heat against my skin. Flames cast light onto the basin Matthew held. Brightness filled my sight— *No. Not now.* This was no time for visions. I tried to turn away, but it was too late. I had no choice but to see—

Cloaked figures following a river toward a town. One of them—a girl my age in a cloak the bright green of mulberry leaves—hesitated a moment, drawing back her hood to reveal long clear hair and bright silver eyes. Faerie eyes, I thought, and then I saw—

Flames consuming the town's houses. Snow sizzled as burning timbers crashed to the ground. Smoke billowed up and I saw—

Ethan watching the houses burn, the clear-haired girl's hand on his arm. She smiled at him, and he smiled back. Neither of them moved to stop the flames. Neither did the younger children arrayed around them. Those flames burned brighter, and by their glow I saw—

Fire leaping from cupped hands to catch at a doorframe. Heat pulsed against my clothes and skin as wood burned—

Metal clattered as the basin hit the ground. Matthew grabbed my arm, and I realized these flames came from no vision. They were real, and they wreathed the doorway to Mom's room.

~ *Chapter 4* ~

Ethan stood amid the flames, fire streaming from his hands to the doorway, from the doorway into the room behind him. The burned-plastic smell of melting nylon filled the air. Smoke billowed around us, clogging my throat as Matthew pulled me farther from the door.

Footsteps pounded up the stairs. Mom ran to us, her body hazy through the smoke. "Get *out*. Both of you." She pushed past to grasp Ethan's nightshirt. His collar burst into flame, and Mom staggered back.

I pulled free of Matthew and grabbed my mother, coughing all the while. Heat burned against my skin. "I'm not going anywhere without you."

Mom fought me. "I won't"—she was coughing, too—"lose another firestarter."

Ethan's sleeves ignited, and flames raced up his

arms. He threw his head back and laughed. Mom struggled toward him, though Matthew, too, had hold of her now.

I wouldn't lose her. *"Mom. Tara. Come here."* Mom stiffened in my grasp. *"Come with me, Mom."* I choked on the words, but I felt the power in them. I dragged her down stairs I could barely see through the smoke, and this time she didn't fight me. She couldn't fight, not while my magic held her. Matthew staggered after us as we ran through the living room and into the open air. Cold slammed into me as I stumbled outside and down a shorter set of stairs. I drew gasping breaths.

Mom fell, coughing, to her knees just a few feet from the house. I crouched beside her. Smoke billowed from our upper windows and drifted over pink clouds that streaked the twilight sky. Matthew and I helped Mom to her feet. She took a step toward the house, then stopped, trembling. My magic held her still. Her back went rigid. "Let me go."

Through the smoke, the windows glowed with orange light. I wasn't about to let Mom back in there. *"Stay here, Mom."* I left her with Matthew and ran toward the open door.

"Ethan!" My throat was raw with smoke and calling. I wasn't sure he would hear, but I felt a cold thread of power pulsing between us once more. *"Ethan, come here!"*

Ethan burst through the doorway and down the outside stairs, his nightshirt aflame. Matthew ran past me, threw him to the ground, and rolled him in the snow. Ethan wept as the flames went out, and the magic between us snapped so fast I stumbled.

Snow began to fall. Ethan gasped and staggered to his feet, his charred nightshirt falling away from his unburned skin. His gaze focused on the orange glow in the windows. "Not again," he whispered, and he raised his blistered, bleeding hands to the sky.

Fire burst through the windows. It flowed, like a molten waterfall, toward Ethan's palms, and it sank through his skin the way water soaked into dry earth. All at once, the fire went out. Ethan took a single step forward and fell, face-first, into the snow.

His back and arms, which had been unharmed moments before, were now a mess of red blisters and fire-blackened skin. Snowflakes sizzled as they hit his charred flesh. Matthew and I tried to sit him up. He groaned and curled away from us, pulling his bleeding hands over his head. Kate ran to us with a blanket.

I was suddenly aware of the townsfolk ringed around us. They carried water buckets and ladders, as if ready to try to put the fire out. A short distance away, Hope's little sister stared at the house, hands outstretched. Hope tapped the younger girl's shoulder, and she let her hands drop. The snow stopped. Hope's sister was a waterworker. She'd been trying to put the fire out, too.

Only there was no fire, not anymore. Kate looked at Ethan, frowned, and drew the blanket away, spreading it on the ground in front of him. The boy's chest was blackened as well, and the touch of wool on his burns would hurt him more than the cold. A burned-meat smell drifted through the air, strong as the smell of charred wood from my house.

"Let me go, Liza." Mom's voice came from behind me. I'd forgotten she stood there, my magic yet holding her. I turned. Her hands and face were blackened with soot, and her sweater was damp with melting snow.

"Let me go so I can see to him." Mom's voice shook.

She was all right. I let out a long breath and felt the magic between us fall away. Mom stumbled forward; I caught her. She flinched as if she were the one who'd been burned.

"Mom?"

She backed away, eyes wide and frightened. "Not you, Lizzy. Please not you." Her shoulders trembled as she knelt by Ethan's side, and I knew I'd get no thanks for saving her.

"You should have let the house burn," she whispered to the boy. "You shouldn't have taken the fire into yourself."

Was that what Ethan had done? He moaned. Was that why the fire he'd called out of our house had burned him, while having his clothes aflame had not?

"So this is your stranger." Brianna's voice was harsh. I looked up and saw that Kyle's mother stood with the rest of the Council, watching us.

Kate stood to face them. Mom kept whispering to Ethan. She wouldn't meet my eyes. What was wrong with her?

From among the townsfolk, others moved to stand with us, dim figures in the fading light: Hope and her husband and her little sister. Seth and his younger sister. Charlotte, who was a year older than me. Other Afters a year or two younger—all but Kyle's brother, Johnny.

Brianna looked at our house. "I assume this fire was caused by magic?"

Mom looked to Kate. Kate nodded, and Mom got to her feet. "It was," Mom said.

Matthew and the other Afters formed a protective ring around Ethan. I crouched by the boy's side, whether to guard him or because I wasn't ready to stand with them, I wasn't sure. It wasn't safe to keep Ethan in our town, not now that we'd seen what his fire could do. Yet if I hadn't used my magic on him, his magic might not have slipped beyond his control. This was my fault, too.

Hope's mother, who'd joined the Council after Father

had left, looked from Brianna to the circle of Afters. "We can't possibly let this child stay here." Hope's mother had forced Hope's little sister out of the house when she'd learned of her waterworking; the girl lived with Hope and her husband now.

"Three days," said Charlotte's dad, who'd been on the Council since before I was born. He was our town's carpenter, and he hadn't kicked Charlotte out of the house when he'd learned of her woodworking magic; he'd declared her his apprentice instead. "We agreed to let the stranger stay three days."

Brianna made a disbelieving sound. "That was before we saw the harm he could do."

Matthew growled softly and clenched his fists. Wind swirled the snow at Hope's feet.

"We're not killers of children." Kate spoke with the same quiet conviction I heard from Matthew sometimes. "Not anymore."

"Looks like Jayce gets the deciding vote." Charlotte's dad chuckled softly. "As usual."

Jayce ran a hand over his bald head and looked to Kate. "You're willing to take responsibility for this boy?"

"Absolutely," Kate said.

Jayce leaned on his cane. "Three days, then," he said. Brianna gave him a withering look.

Ethan began shivering. We needed to get him out of

the cold. "He won't be ready to go anywhere in three days," Kate said.

"That's as close as we're likely to get to a fair compromise. It will have to serve." Jayce glanced at our burned house, then at Mom. "Let us know if there's anything you need, Tara." Mom nodded.

The last of the light had left the sky, and yellow moonlight shone through layers of cloud. The townsfolk began breaking up into smaller groups. Kate turned back to us. "Let's get him inside."

"No way in *hell* they're sending him away," Hope muttered.

"He'll stay with Matthew and me for now." Kate laid a hand on Mom's shoulder. "You and Liza will stay with us, too. Your place isn't in any shape to sleep in tonight."

Mom sighed. "I'm honestly not sure it's safe for Ethan to be in anyone's home."

Kate pressed her lips together. "Only until we can clear out the shed. I'm no fool, Tara."

"I know." Mom smiled wearily. "You're the least foolish person I know. If you and the children can handle getting Ethan moved, I'd best see to the house. Come with me, Liza. We have to talk."

"Yes. We do." We had to talk about how Mom needed to stop putting her life at risk. I followed her to the house, while behind me, Kate asked Matthew to get a stretcher. The temperature was dropping, and cold bit my ears and bare fingers.

Mom disappeared inside, but I stopped when I heard Charlotte's cane tapping the snow, with a lighter sound than Jayce's cane made. She'd lost her leg below the knee the year our town had tried to grow tomatoes, back when we were toddlers. Charlotte had crafted her wooden replacement leg herself, using, I now knew, her magic. It fit so well that beneath her pants and boots, the two legs looked almost alike.

Charlotte gestured toward the house. "Dad and I will take a look in the morning, see if we can't fix the damage."

"Thank you," I said.

Charlotte ducked shyly beneath her curtain of black hair. As children we'd been friends, but then she'd drawn away from me, afraid, she'd said later, that she wouldn't be able to hide her magic from me otherwise. "Afters stick together," she said, just as Seth had, only from Charlotte it sounded like an apology.

I didn't know how to answer it. "I'd better help Mom," I said, and went in.

The living room stank of smoke. Mom walked around it, untacking the nylon over the windows. In one hand, she held a glowing rock, no doubt lit by Seth's sister, whose magic was for calling light to stone. The rock cast eerie purple light on the smoke that lingered in the air around us. Many of the townsfolk still hesitated to use stones such as this, fearing, as I'd once feared, to touch any stone that glowed.

The coals in the fireplace were dead, the house as cold inside as outside. I opened the kitchen shutters to let more smoke out. Mom finished in the living room, found her coat draped over the couch, and pulled it on. We didn't speak as I followed her up the stairs. The railings were cool to the touch. Ethan had left no hint of heat behind when he took the fire into himself.

In the hallway the smell was worse, not only of wood smoke and burned wool but also the melted-plastic stench of burned nylon. There were scorch marks on the walls, and ash dusted the floor. The soot was thicker in Mom's room, and the walls were streaked with black burn marks. I removed what remained of the melted window coverings, and smoke drifted out the windows.

Mom set the glowing stone down on the dresser, against the far wall, which hadn't burned. She opened a drawer, lifted a nightgown, and sniffed it. "This will all need airing." She sighed and opened another drawer, reaching beneath a pile of wool socks and long underwear to pull something out. A silver disk, laced with narrow veins—Caleb's quia leaf. She clutched it and the chain it hung from in one hand, shutting her eyes as if the thing pained her.

"Liza." Mom sat down on the edge of the bed. The purple light gave her eyes a sunken look. "I need your word you won't use magic on me ever again."

Wind gusted through the open windows, sending icy shivers down my neck. "You could have died here."

Mom rocked back and forth, not looking at me. "If you cannot promise not to compel me with your magic, perhaps it'd be best if you leave and let Karinna teach you, because I'm not sure I can."

"*What?*" My hand gripped the windowsill, and charcoal crumbled between my fingers. I released the wood and paced the room. "You're not sending Ethan away. Why does everyone else always matter more than me?"

Mom choked on an indrawn breath. "Is that what you think? Oh, Lizzy . . ." She reached for me, but she still wouldn't meet my eyes. I wanted to let her stroke my hair and whisper my problems away—but the problems had never gone away, no matter what she did.

"Nothing matters more to me than you, Lizzy." Mom's voice was hoarse.

I stopped pacing and stared at the purple stone on the dresser. My father's knife lay beside it, unsheathed. "First you teach the others, but not me," I said, my own voice near breaking. "Then you talk about sending me away. What else am I to think?"

"I'm sorry, Liza, but I won't have my will subject to

someone else's magic. I can't do this again, not after . . ." Her voice trailed off as I turned to her, and her fingers tightened around the leaf.

I return all your choices back to you, Caleb had said. He'd saved Mom's life—but that had been later. In my vision, Mom had run from him. She'd been so afraid.

More oaths. More bindings. Beneath my coat, my sweater felt clammy against my skin. "What did Caleb do?"

Mom looked down, as if ashamed. "No more than all his people did, Before." Smoke drifted through the room. "Glamour, they called it. All faerie folk have it, though none of our human children with magic seem to. The faerie folk used it on us without thought, as easily as breathing, more easily than the magics they had to be taught. I'd not understood how akin to glamour your own magic was until I stood outside my own home, powerless to take a single step to help the child burning within." Mom swallowed. "Glamour's in some of the old books from Before. I should have known better. But once I caught my first glimpse of Faerie, I couldn't let it go. I wanted magic so badly. I'm lucky Kaylen found me. Some of the others weren't as gentle with their human captives."

"Captives?" My voice was too small to bridge the space between Mom and me. In my vision, Karin had called Mom a captive, too.

Mom's laugh was bitter. "All of us who found our way through to Faerie became captives. My father tore the city apart looking for me, but he had no idea how far I'd gone, not until later, and then—" Mom's shoulders slumped. I wanted to put my arms around her, to say she didn't have to tell me any of this.

But I wanted answers too badly. I said nothing. When Mom spoke again, her voice was strained. "I once watched a faerie lord command a human girl to throw herself into a river—and she did it, her eyes on him all the while, laughing right up until the rushing water clogged her throat."

"Caleb wouldn't—"

"No." Mom shut her eyes, seeing things I couldn't. "He watched, though, and made no move to stop it. So I had to watch with him. I think I laughed as well. Glamour is like that. It convinces you everything of theirs is so damned beautiful. There was a boy, the Lady herself turned him into a stag and hunted him like a wild thing. I remember the sound of the horns, the flash of his red flank through the green trees, the way the setting sun outlined his antlers—" Mom's voice tightened around her words. "That was unusual. The Lady can change bodies as well as minds. It's in the nature of her magic. At least with your magic, my mind—my thoughts— remained my own."

Wind blew ash across the room. No one should die like that, with someone else moving their thoughts and limbs. I looked back toward the dresser and Father's knife. I touched the blade. It was sharper than mine.

"At least I was the last," Mom said. "Kaylen lifted his glamour from me in the end, and he gave his word he'd never use it again, on me or anyone else. If grief resulted from that decision in the end, that, at least, wasn't his fault."

"So you forgave him?" Mom hadn't looked anywhere near to forgiving him in my vision.

"I've had time." Mom moved to my side and set Caleb's leaf back inside the drawer. "And I forgave him sooner than he forgave himself. I understand that now. But I would sooner die than have someone else control my thoughts and my actions once more. So I need your word. You must never use your magic on me again."

It was too cold with the windows open. "So long as you're not in any danger, you have my word."

"That's not enough. I know you mean well, Liza, but you truly don't understand."

The fire could have killed her. Did she expect me to just let her die next time? The stone's purple light was dimming. I took it in my hands. "If you don't trust me with my magic, how can you trust any promises I make?"

"It's a funny thing about the faerie folk." Mom

shut the drawer. "They cannot say things they do not mean, and once they give their word, they cannot easily break it."

"But I'm human." I knew well enough that humans could lie.

Mom laughed uneasily. "I've noticed that once the children in this town come into their magic, they develop an odd unwillingness to lie. This has presented challenges in keeping their magic hidden."

No magic controlled my words. I opened my mouth, meaning to tell Mom I wouldn't use my magic to save her life, just to prove I could make false promises as well as anyone.

No words came out. I tried again. My chest tightened, and my breathing went shallow. I couldn't seem to get enough air.

I stopped attempting to speak. Air rushed into my lungs. I gasped, stumbled, and caught myself. I couldn't do it. I really couldn't. I'd always hated to say things that weren't true, but I'd thought it a choice. *My* choice.

"So you can see," Mom said quietly, "why your refusal to give your word makes me uneasy. I'll meet you at Kate's." She turned and left the room.

In my hands the light went out, leaving me in the dark.

✎ *Chapter 5* ✎

My hand clenched the dead stone. How could I refuse Mom, after all she'd been through?

How could she ask such things of me, after all *I* had?

I felt my way down the dark hall to my room. I pulled the coverings off my bedroom windows and took two nightgowns from my dresser, one for me and one for Mom. They smelled faintly of smoke, but there was no helping that. I added clean sweaters, pants, underwear, and socks to the pile. I went back downstairs, pulled on my hat and scarf and gloves, and headed to Kate's.

The path through town was silent now, with just a few faint stars piercing the clouds. Lantern light spilled out around the shutters of the houses and made their tacked nylon glow.

"Sorry about your house, Liza."

I dropped the clothes and spun around, only to find Kyle's brother, Johnny, standing right behind me. He laughed. At fourteen he had a wiry build that made him look taller than he was, along with the wispy beginnings of something no one but him called a mustache on his upper lip.

I hadn't heard him coming. I never did. "Don't *do* that," I said darkly.

Johnny shrugged. His magic was stalking, meaning he was the only human I knew who walked as silently as faerie folk did.

"Don't go spooking the caller, Johnny." Hope's steps crunched toward us through the snow. "That can get you in all sorts of trouble. Almost as much trouble as spooking *me*."

Johnny slouched down in his fur-lined denim jacket. "I'm not afraid of a little wind."

"You should be." Hope helped me pick up the dropped clothes. She sniffed at a sleeve. "We'll find better for you and your mom," she said to me.

"I don't mind." As I folded the clothes, Johnny disappeared the way he'd come, without a sound.

"Everyone else will, if you walk around smelling like this." Hope laughed, and acorns clattered around her face. "Seriously, it isn't any trouble. I was already planning to come by later to check on the firestarter." She

walked with me halfway to Kate's house before peeling
off for her own.

Johnny appeared again at my elbow. "I really am
sorry about the fire."

I flinched but kept walking, as if I'd known he was
there all along. Johnny stopped to scratch at the leg of his
pants. *Kyle's ants,* I thought, and wasn't sorry. I hoped
the leather kept them warm. I hoped they stayed a good
long time.

As far as I could tell, Johnny didn't follow me any
farther. I glanced into Kate's backyard as I neared her
house. Light glowed from within the shed, and tools and
scraps of wood and metal lay on a tarp beside it. They
must have already gotten Ethan inside.

I'd head out there soon, too, but first I crossed
Kate's front porch and entered the warmth of her living
room. I set the damp clothes down near the fireplace,
where a pot of water boiled above the coals. Kate's walls
were covered with bright wall hangings; I glanced at
the one that hid her mirror. Most mirrors had been destroyed during the War, out of fear that the faerie folk
could step through them into our world, but this one
was a family heirloom, so Kate had secretly kept it. No
faerie folk had found their way through the silvered
glass, but I had used the mirror to bring Mom home
from Faerie.

I heard voices from Kate's kitchen.

"What he really needs is a burn clinic," Kate said. Adults were always wishing for medicines and facilities from Before. The way they talked, it used to be that any hurt could be cured, no matter how severe.

"Well, we don't have one." Matthew's voice was quieter—angrier. "That's why I have to go."

I put my hat and gloves in my pockets and joined them. "Go where?" Matthew and I drew each other into a quick hug. He smelled of smoke, too.

"To Caleb and Karin's town," he said as we drew apart. "Ethan—it's bad."

Kate drew a jar from a cabinet. Ground valerian root—it was a sedative, used when pain became too much to bear. "Bad enough I was debating between this and something rather more deadly," she said.

"If Caleb can heal him, it won't come to that," Matthew told her. As far as I could tell, Caleb's healing magic was as powerful as anything from Before.

I tried to picture Caleb controlling Mom's thoughts. He'd risked so much for her—if not for my vision, I might not have believed it, even now, though I knew he was as capable as anyone of pushing too far.

Matthew and I followed Kate to the fireplace, where she sprinkled the valerian root into the pot. I wrinkled my nose as its sweaty-sock smell filled the air. Kate said herbs hadn't worked nearly as well Before as now. I wondered if that meant they'd at least smelled better then.

Strands of soot-smudged hair fell into Matthew's face. "Three days isn't much time. If we can't stop the Council from sending Ethan away, he'll die out there. If Caleb can't come, maybe Allie can." As Caleb's student, Allie didn't know as much about healing as Caleb, but she still could do more than any of us.

My hands and sleeves were streaked with ash. "I thought you didn't intend to let the Council send Ethan away."

"Even if we stop the Council, he'll probably die as he is now," Matthew said. "I can't let that happen, not when I have another choice."

Kate stared into the boiling water. "At least wait until morning."

I thought of Ethan's blackened skin. I wasn't sure a burn like that *could* heal on its own. "Matthew's right. We should go tonight." Once I wouldn't have dared venture out so far into the dark if I had a choice, but that was before the trees slept.

Downy gray wolf fur shadowed the backs of Matthew's hands, a sign he was uneasy. "I'll go faster alone. It would take us all night to reach Caleb's town on foot, but as a wolf I can get there in a couple hours if I run. If Caleb's willing, he could be back here by morning."

"I don't like it," Kate said.

I didn't like it, either. "If anyone should take risks for Ethan, it should be me," I said. Matthew had warned me not to push the firestarter too far.

"But I'm the one best able to do something about it this time." Matthew rubbed the scar on his wrist. "You're not the only one who can save people, Liza."

"I never said—" The words caught in my throat. I'd spent enough time patrolling with Matthew to know he could manage a couple of hours alone in the winter forest well enough. Unless he ran into owls, or wild dogs—I swallowed a nervous laugh. If anyone could handle wild dogs, it was Matthew. "If you're not back by first light, I'll come after you." *We keep each other safe.*

"I'll be back before dawn," Matthew promised. "I'll run ahead of Caleb and Allie whatever they say, so that you'll know whether to expect them."

"I've trusted you before to know where you were needed and to take no more risk than you had to." Kate filled a mug from the pot as she spoke. "I'll have to trust to it now, too, however much I might wish things otherwise. Come. Let's check on Ethan—and tell Tara—before you go."

Matthew shook his head. "Tara will try to stop me. You know that."

Kate drew the mug close, as if for warmth. "I do

know. Perhaps I was hoping for it, and that isn't fair of me, is it?" She set the mug down, brushed a few wisps of gray from her face, and hugged him. "It's nearly spring. Keep an eye out for crocuses. Let me know if you spot any."

"I'll be careful." Matthew knew as well as I the danger crocuses held. Until this year, they'd grown even in winter, burning through leather and wool and the skin of those unfortunate enough to miss them hiding beneath the snow. He pulled away from his grandmother and grabbed my hands. I squeezed them hard. As I looked into his gray eyes, it was all I could do not to pull him closer. I feared if I did, I wouldn't let go and Matthew would lose more time. Besides, Kate stood right beside us, and what if I didn't stop at holding?

Matthew laughed softly. "Nothing to pack—I couldn't carry it anyway." He released my hands to step back, and silver light flowed over him. Skin stretched and changed, arms and legs and body all giving up their shape, as if the form Matthew had worn all his life were illusion, nothing more. He fell to all fours, skin shifting to silver-gray fur, hands and feet to paws with dark pads. Dark markings emerged around his eyes and muzzle and ears. Those ears tilted toward me.

I caught my breath. No matter how often I watched, I never got tired of this. I leaned down and put my arms around him. His fur had grown so thick this winter. I inhaled its musky scent. The smell of smoke was faint now. "Be careful out there," I whispered. "Give Allie a hug for me."

Matthew nudged my chest with his damp nose. He licked my chin, then turned and trotted for the door. I followed, stepping around pants and sweater, boots and wool underwear. I never could seem to catch the moment when his clothes were cast aside.

He stopped by the door and looked up at me. I laughed. Whenever we set out together, I had to open the door. As I turned the knob, Kate moved to my side. We watched together as Matthew made his way across the porch and down the steps. When he reached the path through town, he burst into a loping run. The moon was hidden by cloud, and he quickly disappeared into the dark.

Kate squeezed my shoulder. "I'm going to see to Ethan." She went inside, gathered up her coat and the mug, and left. I lingered on the porch, staring out into the night, for a long time before I followed.

When I did, I found Kate outside the shed, talking with Hope. Hope's little sister grinned beside them as she shifted from foot to foot for warmth. "I get to stay," she announced.

Who better than a waterworker to have around a

firestarter? Hope ruffled her sister's fur cap. "Not alone. The rest of us will take turns with you. Keep guard, in case anyone decides they want Ethan leaving ahead of schedule. You too, right, Liza?"

"Of course." I couldn't run as fast as a wolf, but I could keep watch.

"Good." A gust of wind tugged at the edge of the tarp. Hope absently held out a hand, stilling it. I slid the shed's metal door open and went inside. More glowing stones lit the small space. Orange this time, they provided heat as well as light. Mom sat in a rusted folding chair, watching over Ethan.

He lay on an old army cot. More blisters had burst, and fluid seeped from his skin. There were no blankets around him now. I wondered how he even stood the touch of the soft sheet at his back. Only his face looked peaceful, eyes shut in sleep. His breathing was ragged, though, and the burned-meat smell lingered, along with a faint sickroom scent that made me suspect his wounds had become infected.

Mom looked up, then flinched, as if she feared my magic still.

"How is he?" I asked.

"Holding on." Mom forced herself to look at me. "I don't know how, but he is."

There was no other chair, just a water bucket wedged

into one corner beside a wobbly table. I slid the door shut to keep in the heat. "If all goes well, Caleb will be here by morning. He only need hold on until then."

"Kate told me." Mom frowned. "I wish Matthew hadn't gone."

My back stiffened against the hard metal door, though some part of me wished the same thing. "He only does what needs doing."

"I know," Mom said. "That doesn't stop me from worrying."

"I worry about you, too, you know." It felt good to say so aloud.

Mom said nothing. How much had she not said through the years?

"Did you mean what you told me? About you and Caleb starting the War? Who *were* you?"

"The children of powerful people, Liza, nothing more." Mom's gaze grew distant, as if she were seeing all the way back to Before.

Ethan moaned and kicked the air. Mom made shushing sounds. She reached out to stroke his forehead, but then her hands moved abruptly to her stomach.

"Mom?"

"I'm all right." She stood and pushed past me to open the door and run outside. I heard her throwing up behind the shed. I wondered what it was like to be able to lie.

Ethan kept thrashing at the air. His moans turned to sobs. I didn't hear when Mom returned to the house. I kept watch, making sure Ethan didn't fall from the bed, but otherwise not touching his damaged skin, until Hope and her sister came to take my place. By the time I returned to Kate's house, Mom was asleep on the couch.

"She'll be fine," Kate said, but Kate had kept secrets from me, too. Once Caleb was through healing Ethan, I'd ask him to look at Mom. He'd know whether she was really all right, and, unlike Mom, he wouldn't be able to lie about it.

In Kate's house, as in mine, the downstairs rooms were warmer than the upstairs ones, so in winter everyone slept by the fire. Kate slept in her oversized armchair, while I wrapped myself in blankets on the floor. I kept drifting off only to wake whenever I thought I heard Matthew's paws on the stairs. It was a long time before I slipped into deeper sleep.

When I did, I dreamed of flames roaring around me, of skin melting from my bones. Burning ash clogged my throat, choking my screams. "All human things must die," a stranger's voice said, and I knew I had no choice but to let the fire consume me.

I couldn't let it consume me. I ran, and blistering heat gave way to a cold gray winter forest. A dark shadow lifted its head, and it wore my mother's face. "Liza," the shadow whispered.

I ran harder. I knew if I looked at that shadow again, Mom would be gone, and only the shadow would remain.

"Liza!" Mom called me again and again. "Liza, wake up."

My eyes shot open. I bolted upright, blankets tangling around me. Mom sat beside me—she was real, not a shadow. "You're all right," I said.

Mom reached for me, her eyes seeking mine to make sure I was awake. We'd learned that if she touched me—if anyone touched me—before I fully woke from a nightmare, I'd lash out with my magic, not hearing those around me.

I threw myself into her arms, and she held me close. "I don't want to lose you." I choked on the words and began to cry.

"I know, Lizzy." Mom sounded near tears, too. "I know." She stroked my hair, as if I were still a child, and I let her.

The front door opened. Kate's footsteps crossed the room. Pale light crept in the cracks around the windows.

First light. I was suddenly as wide awake as if someone had poured snowmelt down my back. I pulled away from Mom.

"Where's Matthew?" I asked her.

⌐ *Chapter 6* ⌐

He hadn't come back. I knew it even before Mom said so. Kate thought maybe he'd waited to return on foot with Caleb and Allie after all, but the shadows around her eyes told me she was worried, too. Matthew could no more lie than I could. He had to have meant it when he'd said he would run ahead of the healers.

While Mom tried to talk me into waiting longer, Kate helped me pack. Hope had left clothes for us. I rolled up the sleeves of a borrowed sweater and the legs of a pair of pants, and I packed another set of clothes in the backpack Kate gave me. I also packed dried meat, flint and steel for a fire, a couple of water skins, and oil and cloth for a torch. I stashed more meat in my coat pockets.

"At least take someone with you," Mom said. She'd

not complained when Matthew went alone. Matthew hadn't given her the chance to.

There was no one for me to take. Hope shouldn't be traveling too far, on account of the baby; Seth had three younger siblings he was looking after; and Charlotte couldn't keep the pace I intended to set. I wouldn't risk any of the younger children, not when I didn't know what danger we might face.

Mom stirred the coals with a metal poker. "I can go with you."

"No!" The word came out with more force than I intended. I tied my pack firmly shut. "Not when you're ill."

The words hung between us as the coals burst into flame. Kate pressed a square of cornbread into my hands. I ate it, not wanting to take too much from her rations but knowing I'd need energy for the journey.

"I'm well enough to travel," Mom said.

The fire's heat burned against my face as I buttoned my coat, tied my scarf, and put on my hat and gloves. "It didn't work out very well the last time you decided to travel, did it?"

Mom drew a sharp breath. "Why not dig the knife a little deeper, Liza? You always were good with knives." Mom carefully set the poker down by the hearth. "I know well enough all the ways in which I've failed you. You need not remind me of them."

"I didn't mean—" I couldn't say it. I'd meant every word I'd spoken, and Mom knew it.

"I'd best check on Ethan." She crossed the room and left without another word.

"She's *not* well enough to travel," I said.

"I know." Kate offered me another square of bread, but I shook my head. "Your mother knows, too—but that doesn't mean she has to like it, does it?" She pulled me into a hug. "Bring him home safe, Liza."

"I'll do all I can." I had no trouble speaking that truth. I tied my belt around my coat, slipped my knife into its sheath, and hefted the pack onto my shoulders. My foot nudged something on the floor—the leather tie Matthew used to pull his hair back. It still smelled faintly of wolf and smoke. I knotted it around my wrist.

Kate followed me to the door. Outside, flurries fell from the predawn sky. I stopped at my house to get my bow and a quiver of arrows. The smoke was gone, but its stench lingered as I climbed the stairs.

Mom had lied again: she hadn't gone to Ethan after all. She sat in her room, holding Caleb's silver-plated leaf. At the sound of my steps, she walked into the hall and silently offered it to me.

I shook my head. That leaf had played some small role in whatever had happened between Mom and Caleb. It had nothing to do with me.

"Caleb told me once this would protect me in dark forests." Mom seemed pale in the thin morning light. "I'd keep you out of the dark entirely if I could, but as you like to remind me, I have precious little power to do that. Let me do this much."

I didn't stop Mom as she draped the leaf over my head. "I won't force you to struggle with thanking me," she said, "or with saying anything else you don't mean. Just come back safely. We'll talk then."

I fled into my room, tucking the leaf beneath my shirt as Mom's footsteps descended the stairs behind me. I tied my bow and quiver to my pack, and I took a map I'd copied, too. Neither Matthew nor I had ever taken the direct route between our town and Caleb's town— Washville—but it looked clear enough, a mostly straight road broken only by a few spur trails, one of which led to Ethan's town of Clayburn.

Outside, the sky was gray, the sun below the horizon. Flurries drifted around me, and cold bit through the toes of my boots. I found Matthew's wolf tracks in the snow and followed them to the edge of town. Beyond the last of the ruined houses, his tracks turned to follow the river for a time, and a second set of tracks joined them. Small human boot prints, newer than Matthew's paw prints, wound back and forth across them. A child, and one who'd left only a few hours ago.

One of ours, or another stranger? Both sets of tracks continued alongside the river. I followed them, alert for any sound, quieting my own steps as much as the snow would allow. I scanned the forest for shadows, but there was already too much light. Like tree shadows, most human shadows preferred the dark.

Bare gray and brown trunks rose to either side of the path. A sparrow called out from a high branch, its song small and thin in the chilly morning. In one spot, the child had stopped to make snow angels; in another, he or she had scrambled down to look at something by the river and returned several dozen paces on. In places, the smaller prints were oddly shaped, as if the child had been kicking the snow.

The path veered away from the river, widening into a dirt road. Patches of brown earth and dead leaves showed through where the snow had melted, along with chunks of broken black rock from Before. I kept walking, settling into the relaxed awareness I used on the hunt. Other paths branched off the one I followed, but the prints continued toward Washville as the hours passed and morning gave way to afternoon.

A woodpecker rapped a tree, digging for beetles. The sound echoed through the forest. I stopped, scanning the trees for the bird's red head feathers. Woodpeckers made little distinction between wood and flesh and would peck through human skin in their search for food. The bird was a ways behind me, though, and seemed focused on its tree; for now it posed little threat. I started walking again, then stopped and looked back.

There was an extra set of prints in the snow that hadn't been there before, beside the child's prints and Matthew's and mine. Only a few yards away, the new prints turned toward the forest. I put my hand to my knife's hilt and retraced my steps. I heard no one, but the prints in the snow couldn't lie. Whoever had followed me, his or her steps made no sound. The only people I knew who could walk that quietly were Karin and Caleb and—

"Johnny, get out here. Now." I kept my voice low, not wanting to attract the woodpecker's attention.

Someone coughed softly behind me. I spun around, drawing my knife and taking a step back as I did. Johnny stood there, grinning. "You *are* predictable, Liza."

I closed the distance between us without lowering my blade. "I told you not to do that."

Johnny shrugged and hunched down in his jacket. His knife hung from a belt underneath it. "You also told me to reveal myself."

I sheathed my knife and stalked past him. "Go home." Surely he had better things to do than make trouble here.

I didn't hear him following, but I saw, this time, when Johnny came up beside me. "Funny thing—I'm actually heading the same way you are today."

"Hilarious." A dragonfly thrummed ahead of us down the road, clutching a firefly between its legs. The dragonfly's wings shone green, while the firefly pulsed a colder yellow. "Brianna won't be happy to find you missing."

"And you're supposed to be so good at paying attention." Johnny slipped out of sight between one breath and the next. "Anyone can tell it's a relief to my mom when she can't see me. My magic makes things easier for her."

The firefly shimmered. Its yellow light licked the air and caught the dragonfly's veined wings, running along them like liquid fire. The larger insect quivered. There was a small, bright flash, and then the dragonfly dissolved into lacy ash.

The firefly flew off, still glowing. I focused on the path and Matthew's tracks. If Johnny chose to go walkabout, that was no concern of mine. I'd waste no more breath on it.

The snow grew softer and wetter, and the brown patches of dirt and leaves grew more frequent. As the afternoon temperature edged above freezing, I put my gloves and hat into my pockets. Clouds thickened around me, and a crow's harsh caw cut the air. I scanned the forest but saw no sign of the black birds. Crows blended readily into the dull winter trees, as if they had stalking magic of their own.

The crow called out again. Crows were scavengers, with little skill for bringing down prey, but they'd been known to peck out the eyes of live animals from time to time. I came to another spur path, the one that led to Clayburn. Matthew's wolf prints and the child's boot prints both turned onto that narrower trail. Matthew had stopped running. His steps were more deliberate, rear paws placed carefully into the tracks left by front ones, as if something had made him cautious. Beside his prints, the child's showed no such hesitation.

I moved my hand to my knife as I followed them, knowing that Matthew wouldn't have left the road without cause. Gray ash dusted the snow. A burned smell crept into the air, with a cooked-meat edge that reminded me of Ethan's burns. Matthew would have smelled it sooner than I did. Had he gone to investigate? I slowed my steps. I hoped that if Johnny was still here, he was being careful, too.

A shard of white bone poked through a patch of snow. More bones lay exposed against brown earth, burned flesh clinging to them. Human bones: a thigh, a shattered kneecap, two fingers. My hand tightened around the knife's hilt. The bones were too small to have come from adults.

I heard Johnny draw breath between his teeth, though I still couldn't see him. More burned bones littered the path and forest as I walked on, most already picked over by scavenging birds or dogs. I gagged on the scent of dead flesh. Had Ethan's magic killed them, just as it had killed Ben? Had I made a mistake, leaving Mom and Kate and the Afters to watch over Ethan without me?

Matthew's prints grew deeper, as if he'd stopped entirely. A second set of prints—adult-sized and barely breaking the snow—appeared, and wolf and human continued on together, while the child's newer prints followed. Why hadn't Matthew turned back? There was nothing he could do here, and he'd wasted time Ethan might not have.

In the distance, a child spoke softly. Around a bend, the path gave way to a churned-up mess of ash and bone and mud. Kyle knelt in the muck, talking to a bird perched on a child's skull, a scrap of flesh dangling from its beak.

Johnny ran past me to kneel beside his brother. Kyle looked up at him, then turned back to the bird. A slick of the younger boy's hair stuck up, because of course he'd forgotten his hat.

"He's hungry." Kyle's face was smudged with mud and ash. "It's not the bird's fault that he's hungry."

"I know." The gentleness in Johnny's voice surprised me. "You ready to come home, kid?"

Kyle didn't answer.

"You went after him," I said to the older boy.

Johnny didn't look away from his brother. "Somebody had to."

A wind picked up, blowing ash toward us. The crow looked up from the skull, which was missing its two front teeth.

"*Go away,*" I commanded the bird. With an angry rustling of feathers, it flew to a high branch that hung over the path.

"He's not happy." Kyle wiped his face on his sleeve, smearing ash across his nose. He wasn't wearing gloves, either.

I crouched by his other side. "Kyle, what are you doing here?"

"Running away," he said as if it were the most obvious thing in the world.

"Third time this month," Johnny muttered. "And the farthest he's managed to get yet." He reached for Kyle's hand, but Kyle stuck out his lower lip and shook his head. Could I use my magic to send him all the way home?

The crow cawed from its branch. "Look out!" Kyle yelled.

Johnny and I grabbed our knives as other crows answered from the trees all around us. Wing beats pounded the air as the birds attacked.

My blade grazed a black wing. A sharp claw scraped my cheek. *"Go away!"* I commanded.

"Go 'way, go 'way, go 'way!" Kyle echoed.

"Get down!" Johnny shouted at him.

My blade drew blood this time, and a crow dropped to the ground. The others whirled and took to the sky. I stepped back, panting, as the birds became black specks against gray clouds. How hungry did they have to be to attack us all at once?

"I told *them*." Kyle lifted his chin.

I sheathed my knife. Just then I didn't care who Kyle thought had sent the birds away, as long as they were gone.

Johnny grabbed his brother's hand. "Time to go, kid. I mean it."

Kyle shook his head. I wiped blood from my cheek and looked around, scanning the trees. If more crows lurked there, they blended with bark and branch as well as before. Sunlight forced its way through the clouds, reflecting off something shiny at my feet. A child's silver bracelet, with dangling charms: a heart, a key, a cat. I reached for it.

The bracelet shone brighter, too bright for the gray afternoon. Silver light filled my sight and I saw—

A girl my age with long clear hair standing on the trail, where charred flesh yet clung to the bones around her. She gazed at a woman with hair just as clear bound up in a glimmering net. "I passed your test," the girl said, but the woman frowned, disapproval clear in her silver eyes. "Tell me whether any escaped this time," the woman said, "before you speak of success—"

Karin, looking up at the same woman, speaking the same words: "I passed your test." Only they stood in a deep green forest, and the woman smiled in response. Karin lifted her chin, pride plain enough in her bright eyes—

An elbow jabbed my side, and Johnny hissed under his breath. My fingers closed around the bracelet as the visions fled. A girl stood in front of me, the clear-haired girl I'd just seen—the same girl who'd watched a town burn with Ethan by her side.

I hadn't heard her coming, any more than I'd ever heard Johnny.

∽ *Chapter 7* ᴄ

The girl's green dress and cloak were dusted with ash. So were her battered black boots. Her clear hair was pulled back by a silver butterfly, its bright legs twisted to form the clasp. She stared at us, stiff and straight-backed. I glanced at her silver eyes and knew she was no more human than Karin or Caleb.

Karin and Caleb had taught me not all faerie folk were monsters, but that didn't mean they all could be trusted. I dropped the bracelet and waited, hand within reach of my knife, to see what this stranger would do. Johnny clutched Kyle's hand, the older boy's shoulders tensed.

Kyle frowned. "The butterfly doesn't like it there."

The girl reached around to touch the clasp, and the wings trembled beneath her hand. "It has been there many years, and butterflies are not accustomed to living so long. Would you have me kill it?" The girl spoke with idle curiosity.

What role had she played in the burning of the dead children around us—and why was she the only child from my visions untouched by Ethan's fires? "Who are you?" I demanded.

Johnny rolled his eyes. "Charming as always." The wariness didn't leave him, but he held out his hand. "I'm Johnny. This is Kyle and Liza."

I gave him a sidelong look. I would have kept our names from this stranger, at least until we knew why she was here. Names had power. I'd learned that laying shadows to rest.

"You may call me Elin." The girl absently poked a bone with her boot. There were thorns woven into the hem of her dress and the edges of her sleeves. "Kyle. Johnny. Liza." She turned the words on her tongue. "I think you should come with me." Her voice took on a velvet softness. My skin tingled, as if her words were trying to take root there. Perhaps I'd only imagined it.

Perhaps not. I knew better than to ignore any instinct of danger. I turned toward Johnny, not letting Elin wholly out of my sight. "You should get Kyle home."

"Yeah." Johnny's voice was strange, as if he weren't quite awake. "Yeah, I think you're right." He stepped back, pulling Kyle with him. The younger boy jerked away and threw his arms around Elin's legs.

"Stay with you!" he declared.

Elin looked down as if Kyle were a distasteful insect she'd found in her bedding. She turned to Johnny and me. "You'll both come, too, of course."

Johnny's gaze softened. "Sure. Why not?"

Magic. Nothing else could make Johnny so agreeable. Gooseflesh prickled along my arms. Elin was calling him and Kyle, in some way I didn't understand.

Kyle reached toward Elin's hair. Elin smiled, removed her clasp, and put it into his hands. Her clear hair fell to her waist. The butterfly's silver antennae quivered, and I felt something cold within the clasp reaching for me, begging to be set free.

Kyle smiled and patted the butterfly's wings, as if he hadn't wanted to free it himself moments before. The wings began to flap. "Pretty," he said.

Glamour is like that. Mom's words. *It convinces you everything of theirs is so damned beautiful.* Ice trickled down my spine, and I took a few steps back. *"Johnny. Kyle. Come here."*

Kyle clutched the butterfly in one hand as he walked toward me, dragging his feet. I grabbed his other hand. Johnny slouched, as if he didn't much care whether he listened to me or not, yet I felt the cold thread of my magic between us. "You always take everything so seriously," he complained as he moved to my side.

I grabbed his hand, too. "Come on." *We're getting out of here.* I walked away from Elin, back toward my town. Kyle and Johnny followed; they had no choice. Once I got them safely away, I'd return to find Matthew.

"Kyle," Elin called in her velvety voice.

Kyle kept holding my hand, but he pressed his lips into a pout. "Let me *go*, Liza."

"Kyle, you seem like such a sweet child," Elin crooned. "I would very much like to see the color of your blood. Will you show it to me? The butterfly's pins are sharp enough."

Kyle took the clasp and jabbed it into his arm. Blood trickled out. He lifted the clasp to stab himself again. I dropped Johnny's hand, grabbed the butterfly from Kyle, and flung it into the forest.

Johnny bolted to Elin's side before I could grasp his hand again. She stroked his hair, and he bent toward her, like a well-behaved cat.

"Johnny," I called. *"Come here."*

"Quit it, Liza." His voice, at least, still sounded like his own.

"Johnny!"

He walked toward me, scowling. Even as he did, Kyle jerked free and inched away, a guilty look on his face.

"Kyle!"

Kyle stopped moving away, but Johnny turned back to Elin.

"So you're a summoner, are you, Liza?" Elin placed a possessive hand on Johnny's shoulder. "That's almost as inconvenient as the fact that glamour doesn't seem to touch you. Yet even a summoner only wields so much power, especially when other magics fight her. You cannot hold them both for long. Glamour grows stronger over time."

I didn't need to hold them. Magic flowed in two directions—Karin had taught me that. *"Elin. Go away."*

"Is that the best you can do, Summoner?" Elin's silver eyes filled with disdain. "Johnny, I believe I should like to see your blood as well."

Johnny nodded like a child eager to please. He took his knife from its sheath and brought it to his left wrist.

I ran at him, grasped his right arm just above the knife, and twisted. The blade fell to the ground. I grabbed it and flung it into the forest. A thin line of blood welled up from Johnny's skin, but the cut wasn't very deep. I spun back toward Elin.

Her hands closed around my throat. "I think that will be quite enough, Liza."

As I lurched away, wool tightened around my throat, leaving me gasping for air. My scarf—I grabbed at it but couldn't pull it away. *"Go away, Elin, go away!"* I choked on the words as I reached for my knife. I should have gone for the knife from the start. It couldn't fail me the way magic could.

Elin's hand brushed my wrist. Wool flowed over my fingers, and my own sweater sleeve wrapped around my hand, forcing my fingers into a fist. I reached for the sleeve with my other hand, but I was too slow. Elin grabbed it, and wool flowed over that hand, too, trapping it. I staggered, letting my pack, with its bow and quiver, fall from my shoulders. *"Go away, go away—"* I needed more air. I brought my bound fists to my neck, but they were too clumsy. My sight blurred, and I fell, gasping, to my knees. Kyle laughed. The sound seemed very far away.

Elin's fingers brushed my neck again, and the scarf loosened. I drew gulping breaths as I stumbled to my feet. *"Elin, go away!"* I threw all the power I could into the call.

Elin's laugh was wild. "As if after the Uprising I would entrust any human with my full name. Perhaps if your power were greater or we'd known each other longer, this short form would suffice, but that is no matter." She looked down at me. "And now, Liza, I believe we are ready to talk." She took my knife from its sheath. I lunged at her, but she stepped aside and handed the knife to Kyle. "Kyle, dear, would you hold this?"

I would not let fear cloud my thoughts. I would *not.*
Kyle tested my knife against one finger, but Elin made a
tsking sound. "Not yet." Kyle obediently drew the knife
away. Johnny moved to Elin's other side. My hold on
them was gone.

"Take me if you must, but let Kyle and Johnny go."
I had a chance yet of fighting my way free, but Kyle and
Johnny didn't, not while glamour controlled them.

"I don't think so." Elin's silver eyes were bright.
"Though glamour doesn't touch you, as a weaver I have
power enough of my own, and if it is a small thing beside
my mother or grandmother's magic, still it has its uses.
Give me your hands."

I backed away. "What do you want with us?"

"That is for the Lady to decide. Your hands, Liza."

The Lady will not like this. Karin's words, from my
vision. Mom had spoken of a lady, too, when she'd told
me about glamour. She'd said the Lady had turned a boy
into a stag and hunted him, and her voice had tightened
with fear.

There was a black walnut tree just a few paces from
the path. If I could get to it, tear my sleeves against its
bark—

"This will *not* do." Elin turned to Kyle. "You may
use the knife now."

He pressed the steel to his palm at once, slicing skin.

"Kyle! Come here!"

He shuffled toward me. The blade seemed huge against his small hand. Blood welled up as he pressed it in deeper.

"Give me the knife."

Kyle hesitated, then shook his head—no. He grinned as his hand grew slick with blood. Johnny laughed as he watched us.

A few more steps and I'd reach the tree, but if Kyle cut too deep, he could lose use of his hand. I stopped, drew a sharp breath, and held my hands out in front of me. "Leave him alone."

Elin's feral smile reminded me of a cat that had cornered its prey. "No more playing with the knife, Kyle."

Kyle frowned, but he drew the blade away. So much blood—I couldn't tell whether tendons had been severed. He looked up at me, and for an instant fear flashed across his face. "Hurts," he whispered.

Elin patted his shoulder. "Of course it doesn't hurt."

Kyle nodded slowly, though his hand still bled. Anger threatened to choke me, as surely as my scarf had.

"If you take so much as a single step without my leave, Liza, I shall feel free to command him to slit his own throat. Do you understand?"

"I understand." I kept the fear from my voice. Anger had its uses, after all.

Kyle stared down at his bleeding hand, as if it puzzled him. Elin glanced at Johnny. "Find my butterfly, and bring it back to me." Johnny headed off among the trees to do as she asked while Elin stalked toward me.

"Much better. Grandmother says all humans come into line sooner or later. It is simply a matter of learning to speak your crude language." Elin took my hands in hers. I fought not to flinch as she rolled up my loose coat sleeves and crossed my arms in front of me. Wool flowed once more, liquid and glimmering, until my sweater bound my arms together at the wrists. Elin smiled as she stroked the sleeves, and the rest of the sweater tightened around me, constricting my ribs. I gave a sharp gasp. I could breathe, but I couldn't run. I pulled at my sleeves. The binding at my wrists held. I was trapped.

Panic shuddered through me. Kyle drew his bleeding palm to his mouth, as if his wound were a mere curiosity. "Bind his hand." Talking hurt with the sweater tight around me.

Elin smiled sweetly. "Kyle doesn't mind a little blood, does he?" Kyle shook his head. "Still, it would not do to bring him to the Lady damaged." Elin strode idly to Kyle and touched the sleeve of his wool coat. Light flowed beneath her fingers, and a strip of wool fell away into her hands, as surely as if she'd cut it. She wrapped the cloth around Kyle's injured hand and ran her fingers over the wool. The edges melted together, the way wood melted beneath Charlotte's hands. When Elin drew away, a tight gray bandage circled Kyle's palm. Kyle grinned, even as blood began to seep through.

Johnny returned with Elin's butterfly. The wings were bent, but they flapped on. Elin frowned as she straightened them and drew her hair from her neck. "If you try to use your magic in any way, Liza, there will be more blood. I trust you understand that as well. Do you require that I gag you, or will you behave?"

"I'll—" Words caught in my throat. I couldn't promise to do as she asked if I didn't mean it. "You don't need to gag me."

"Good." Elin took Kyle's bandaged hand. He wrapped his fingers around hers. Johnny reached for her other hand. "You will walk ahead of me, so that I can watch you. Follow the trail."

"Where are we going?"

Elin made a shushing sound. "I have not given you leave to ask questions, Summoner. Do you seek to anger me so soon?"

Johnny tilted his head at me, as if puzzled. "You worry too much, Liza."

"Indeed," Elin said. "Start walking."

I wanted to throw myself at her. I did not want to walk into danger at her command. But I moved forward, my bound gait stiff, my breath tight. If we continued along this path, we'd be heading straight for Clayburn. Rain began to fall in large, cold drops. Elin's steps made no sound, but I heard Kyle behind me. Johnny, too—for once he wasn't using magic to hide himself.

My thoughts remained my own. I held to that, staying alert for any way free of this trap.

We left ash and mud and the picked-over bones of the dead behind. Elin asked Johnny questions: about his magic, and Kyle's, and mine; about the other children in our town. Johnny obediently answered them all.

Raindrops pocked the soft snow and made puddles in the dirt. Matthew's prints continued on, as did the stranger's prints beside them. Wherever Elin was taking us, Matthew had gone that way, too. There'd be no help for Ethan from either of us anytime soon.

The air grew heavy with the scent of dead leaves. Sun poked through the clouds, but it seemed a thin thing beside the damp and the cold. Kyle whined once about being hungry, but at a word from Elin fell silent. I was hungry, too. The dried meat in my pockets might as well have been miles away.

As the sun neared the horizon, it gave off a yellow glow. Light reflected off a puddle ahead of me. I stumbled, the light turned golden bright, and in that brightness I saw—

Matthew, whining as he nosed at the bones of the burned children, not seeing the dark shadow that fell across his path. I tried to cry out a warning, but then I saw—

Karin, reaching into a wall of ivy and hawthorn and briars, the Wall that protected her town. Greenery parted as she cupped her hands around something tangled within—a silver quia leaf on a chain, much like the one Mom had given me. The scene shifted, and green leaves gave way to bare winter branches, but Karin continued holding her leaf. As if in response, my own leaf grew warm against my chest.

"Karin!" I called, knowing better than to expect her to hear, knowing that visions could never wholly be trusted and that it might not be the present I saw.

Yet Karin tilted her head, as if puzzled. Her brows drew together, and her gaze focused right on me. "Liza? What is wrong? Where are you?"

"Near Clayburn—" I wasn't sure if I mouthed the words or spoke them, but as I did, I fell forward.

The puddle splashed beneath me. I looked up, into silver eyes—not Karin's eyes. Elin grabbed my scarf as I struggled to my feet. It tightened around my throat, and dizziness made me stagger. "I'm sorry," I gasped. Under my too-tight sweater, the quia leaf remained warm against my skin. Caleb had said the leaf would protect Mom in dark forests. Could it be protecting me from Elin's glamour, too? "I will do my best"—I drew a strangled breath—"not to fall again."

The scarf loosened as Elin turned away. She laid a hand on Kyle's shoulder. "You may play with the knife again, if you're careful. You do know how to be careful, don't you?"

Kyle nodded and tested the tip of the knife against his bandage. He watched with mild interest as fresh blood soaked through the blood that had clotted there. Johnny watched, too, a dreamy look on his face.

"I said it wouldn't happen again." Anger colored my voice.

"I am aware of that. This was just a reminder that you'd best keep your word. Enough, Kyle." Elin laughed, but it sounded forced. "Isn't Liza silly to fall?"

"Silly!" Kyle grinned at me as if we shared some secret. Johnny rolled his eyes, almost as he might have done without glamour, but then he laughed, too. How could Caleb have ever used magic like this on Mom?

Elin shoved me forward. "Keep walking."

I walked, but something felt different—my sweater, where my wrists were bound, wasn't quite as tight as before. I tugged on it, and the wool gave a little, as if some tear had weakened the fabric when I fell. It felt looser around my ribs, as well.

The rain had stopped. As the sun dipped below the horizon, I slowly worked at the weak spot in the fabric, using movements I hoped were too small to see. Fibers gave way, one by one.

I heard Johnny stumble in the fading light. Kyle complained he was tired, and Elin silenced him by telling him he wasn't. A shadow floated across our path, brushing my leg. I shivered as I felt the longing within it, the cold desire to be called—there was nothing I could do about that now. The shadow floated on. Had it belonged to one of the children Elin had killed? I no longer doubted she'd commanded Ethan to burn them all. I wondered if he'd even understood was he was doing. *Not my fault.* He might be dying for it even now.

Another fiber gave. I uncurled my fingers, curled them again before Elin could see. Wind brushed my face and sent shivers down my spine. A faint burned scent returned to the air, though the wind didn't come from the direction of the dead children. It came from Clayburn.

Wool tore. My wrists pulled away from each other. I pressed them together again, careful not to move too fast. I felt the skin of wrist touching wrist through the holes in the fabric, Matthew's hair tie between them. I inched my fingers up through my sleeves, slowly widening those holes.

"Carry me," Kyle whispered. Elin made a disdainful

sound. When I looked back, it was Johnny who carried Kyle. The younger boy leaned his head sleepily against his brother's shoulder, clutching my knife like a toy he didn't want to let go.

The burned smell grew stronger as we came to the ruined houses that meant we were near the edge of a town. The path continued on, toward pale bluffs that reached for the sky. We veered off it. The forest gave way to cleared land, but the ruins went on. One house's roof had fallen in, and its walls were blackened and crumbling. The next house had burned to the ground, and the one after it, too. A man lay lifeless in the snow, arms flung open, shirt burned away.

I choked on the stench of charred flesh. This wasn't the edge of a town. This was—this had been—Clayburn. *She didn't only kill the children.*

"Smells bad," Kyle muttered sleepily.

"No, it doesn't," Elin told him. Kyle didn't complain again.

We passed a woman whose fingers had melted together where they were folded over her chest, a man whose frost-stiffened hair fell over the sunken sockets of eyes that had burned away. I tasted bile at the back of my throat, even as I wondered why Elin hadn't killed the children here, too, instead of waiting to take them so far beyond the town.

The last of the light left us, and a bright moon poked through the clouds. A great horned owl hooted, a mournful sound.

"Owl's hungry," Kyle muttered. "Me too." Elin didn't bother answering him. The houses grew closer together, some piles of ruined timbers, others half standing. Their blackened beams glistened in the moonlight. More shadows drifted among them, keeping their distance from us, as if dying had taught them, too late, to be afraid.

The holes in my sweater were large enough to get my hands through now. I slowed my steps. I'd go for Elin's eyes—that was my best chance of disabling her without weapons or magic, and it might buy Johnny and Kyle the time to escape.

The wind died. I caught a whisper of movement, and a woman silently stepped out from between two fallen houses.

She wasn't human. I knew it at once, down to my bones, would have known even without her pale hair, piled in braids atop her head and held in a net that glittered with icy green light, or her silver eyes, which shone as bright as moonlight itself. Her long brown dress was frayed at the hem and sleeves, yet she moved in it with a liquid grace that nothing human could hope for. Only her heavy black boots seemed out of place. I felt a fleeting desire to bow before her. The leaf burned hot against my chest.

Kyle stared up at her, rapt, from within Johnny's arms. I couldn't attack her and Elin at the same time. Some part of me didn't want to.

The Lady. Who else could this be? Her smile was filled with sharp edges, like broken glass from Before. She gestured with one hand.

A gray wolf trotted out of the shadows and sat by her side.

∽ *Chapter 8* ∾

*M*atthew. The Lady stroked the top of his head, and he leaned into her touch. If he saw me, he gave no sign.

The quia leaf remained warm, but otherwise every last bit of me felt icy cold. *Not Matthew.* The Lady drew her hand away, and Matthew curled up at her feet. He was under her glamour, as surely as Kyle and Johnny were under Elin's. *No.*

I was staring at him—I forced my gaze away. If they saw that Matthew and I knew each other, that could be used against us. I had to wait, to see what was happening here and what I could do about it. It had never been so hard not to act.

A corner of the Lady's mouth twitched, and I knew I'd already given myself away. Johnny set Kyle down. "Matthew!" Kyle cried, and threw himself at the wolf.

Matthew snarled. Kyle skittered back, and his face scrunched up. "Matthew's never mean."

"He is whatever I command him to be." The Lady reached down and stroked Matthew's fur. "Does the scent of humans trouble you, my pet?" Matthew gave an uneasy half growl.

I pressed my feet against the snow, forcing myself not to leap at her. That would serve no one. When my chance came, though, I'd do worse than go for her eyes. *If only I knew her name.* She wouldn't be standing there at all, then.

Elin stepped forward. "Grandmother," she said. The woman looked no older than Caleb or Karin—but I knew that faerie folk lived longer than humans and did not age as we did.

The Lady's gaze swept over Johnny, Kyle, and me as if we were little more than ants beneath her feet. "These are not the ones who destroyed our people."

Elin looked swiftly down. "I found them where I found the others. It would not have done to leave them there, where they might cause trouble."

The Lady frowned. "Since when does my granddaughter fear the trouble that humans might bring? You saw to the others readily enough, the children who escaped your control and caused such great harm. All but the fire speaker who led them and the child who escaped

with him. I trusted you to deal with them, too, else I
would not have returned to this town, not even to bury
our people."

Ben, I thought. *Ethan.* Elin hadn't waited to kill
the children—they'd escaped, and she'd pursued them.
She must have caught Ethan again for long enough to
make him burn the others, but he'd gotten away in the
end. Was he still alive in our town, waiting for help that
might never come?

"I thought you might have a use for these three." Elin
seemed young beside the Lady, for all that the Lady didn't
look old. "Just as you had a use for the shifter, when we
came upon him. I have brought you a lightfoot, an animal speaker, and a summoner."

The Lady's hair flickered with cold green light.
"What use have *I* for an animal speaker? Dispose of that
one, and I will give some thought to the others."

I edged toward Kyle. Wind tugged at Elin's long hair.
"An animal speaker would be of use to me," she said.

"Your hesitation displeases me." The Lady knelt in
front of Kyle. "Child, I need for you to take that knife to
your heart. It is not a difficult thing—you can do that for
me, can you not?"

Kyle nodded, eager as a puppy chasing a pack. He
lifted the knife.

I ran at him, pushing my hands through my torn

sleeves and grabbing the knife from his hand. I threw it far from us both. The Lady turned to me, her eyes glimmering in the dark, her anger pushing against me like a physical thing.

I reached beneath my sweater, grabbed the leaf from around my neck, and threw it over Kyle's head. *"Run, Kyle! Go away! Go someplace safe!"*

Kyle's eyes went wide as the glamour left him. For a moment I feared he'd burst into tears. Instead he turned and ran toward the path and the bluffs, arms swinging, feet pounding over the snow and mud.

The Lady's cold gaze fell on Elin.

"Allow me to go after him." There was a tremor in the girl's voice. The butterfly in her hair flapped faster, like the trapped thing it was. "I won't hesitate again. I'll catch him, and I'll kill him."

"Oh, you will indeed." The Lady grasped her granddaughter's wrist. Silver light bloomed between her fingers. That light flowed up Elin's arms, down her body—I blinked in the sudden brightness, and when my sight cleared, a red-tailed hawk perched trembling on the Lady's fist, with sharp talons and yellow eyes. Elin's dress and boots and butterfly clasp lay at the Lady's feet. *The Lady can change bodies as well as minds. It's in the nature of her magic.* Mom had told me that, too.

The butterfly half flew, half hopped across the snow.

The Lady brushed her fingers over Elin's feathers. "Pursue the animal speaker. Destroy him, and bring the leaf he bears back to me. Do not return until you have it. We will discuss your failure to control your human captives then."

The Lady lifted her arm. Elin launched silently into the air, brown wings and red tail spread wide. Kyle disappeared beyond the houses, and Elin followed him.

I ran after them, knowing that Kyle couldn't possibly outrun a hawk, knowing I could do little to protect him from one. My torn sweater sleeves flapped in the wind.

I saw a blur of gray. Matthew slammed into my side, knocking me to the ground. I felt his hot breath on my face, his paws on my chest. I looked up, gasping. His teeth were bared, and his eyes held a wildness that reminded me of the crazed dogs he'd once saved me from.

"*Matthew*," I called softly. He shuddered, and for a moment his eyes were Matthew's eyes once more. He whined and backed off me. "That's right, Matthew." I got to my feet, held out my hands. "It's only me, Matthew, only Liza—"

The Lady walked up beside him and put a hand to his back. "Well done, my wolf." All recognition left Matthew's eyes. The Lady scratched him behind the ears, and he flopped down beside her, his tongue hanging out one corner of his mouth.

"Let him go." I kept my voice low, controlled.

The Lady's fingers grasped my wrist. "I don't think so, little Summoner." Her voice was cold, and that cold settled deep inside me. My legs trembled, weak as water, and I knew that the time for running was past.

"How did you come to possess a leaf of the First Tree and first line, Liza?"

The words burrowed down beneath my skin. My lips moved. "My mother gave it to me."

I hadn't meant to speak. Why had I spoken?

"Indeed?" The Lady's fingers brushed my hair. *I have no protection now.*

I wanted no protection. I tilted my face to look into the Lady's bright eyes. Had I noticed before how beautiful she was? Beautiful as the ice storms that coated trees in winter, bringing them down one by one. Her hair glimmered in its net. She had fireflies bound into it, alive as the butterfly Elin had worn. I couldn't stop staring at them. *So pretty.* She smiled, and my fear shivered out of me.

"How did your mother come to possess such a thing?" The Lady's words were sharp as ice, cutting through skin and bone and thought, digging deep inside me for answers.

Her voice *hurt,* the way a knife's blade hurt. I longed to hear it again. "Caleb—Kaylen—gave it to her."

The Lady went utterly still. "Indeed?"

I wanted to kneel at her feet, but she put one hand on my shoulder, fingers digging through my jacket, forcing me to stand. "So Tara yet lives?" She spoke my mother's name as if it tasted bad. I nodded, grateful it wasn't me who'd made the Lady unhappy.

Her fingers dug deeper, surely bruising me, but I didn't mind. I hoped my pain pleased her. The Lady released me, and I fell to my knees. "You will take me to your mother," she said softly. "After my granddaughter kills the boy and retrieves the leaf. We shall all visit Tara then."

The Lady reached down and stroked my cheek, where the crow's claws had scratched it. I shivered at her touch. "You want to see your mother, don't you, Liza?"

"Yes." I wasn't sure quite why I'd left her. "I miss Mom."

"Of course you do. Perhaps when this is through, I shall let you be the one to take her life at last. You would like that, yes?"

Something about the Lady's words didn't make sense, but I couldn't puzzle out what—and I did want to please her. "Of course."

The Lady laughed and took my chin in her hands. "So weak, human minds. You've always been weak.

That the Uprising happened at all is an insult that will be avenged, though the Realm itself winds down. Come with me, Liza."

I stood and wrapped my fingers around hers, trusting as a child. I couldn't remember when I'd last trusted anyone like that.

I'd trusted Matthew, hadn't I? I held out my hand to the wolf, who stood once more. He snarled and drew away, and I wasn't so certain.

The Lady turned slowly around, as if looking for someone else. Johnny, I realized. He wasn't here. Of course he wasn't. "Johnny does that," I said. "Disappears, and hides, and sneaks up on people." I lowered my voice, as if sharing a secret. "I hate him, you know."

The Lady hadn't spoken to Johnny. Only Elin had. He didn't know yet that he needed to obey the Lady, too. I saw his boot prints disappearing through the snow, in the same direction Kyle had gone.

The Lady ran her fingers along Matthew's back. "I trust you can sniff him out, pet? Find him, and bring him back to me."

Matthew barked and trotted off, following Johnny's prints.

I let the Lady lead me away. Wind had scattered the clouds, and moonlight illuminated the bodies of the dead as we walked through Clayburn's ruins. The temperature was dropping, but the stench of smoke and decomposing flesh lingered in the air.

"A sweet scent, is it not?" the Lady asked.

Something twisted inside me, something that needed above all else to please her. The smell grew strange and sweet, like dead flowers. I inhaled deeply and quickened my steps.

"Human towns are weak, too. Every one of them holds the seeds of its destruction within its own children." The Lady's fingers tightened around mine. "Time was that humans had their uses. They were crafters, singers, players, entertaining diversions from life in the Realm. The Uprising swept all that away, when your human weapons held more power than anything human-crafted had a right to. Many of our shelters did not hold, and the injury your weapons dealt our land made it reluctant to yield up sustenance even for those who survived. Still we grew what we could, until this past season, when the land refused to serve us at all." Despair crept into the Lady's voice, as beautiful as the scent of decay. "So we came to your world at last, to take from it what we could. Only your land has proven as gray and desolate as our own. Even humans must know that nothing more can grow out of such death. And so the worlds wind down, and tragedy runs its course."

We walked past the last of the burned houses. Beyond

them, bare trees lined a frozen river. Trees had always slept in winter; the adults in my town all said so. Yet what were the assurances of humans beside the Lady's words? I'd never truly believed that spring would return after this gray season.

The Lady glanced past the river, where the bluffs reached for the sky. "Have no fear, Summoner. The Realm will be avenged before this is through, and your frail human towns will fall, one by one. That is justice, is it not?"

I nodded my agreement as we came to a fallen house at the far edge of town, one that wasn't burned, only broken, beams and planks sticking out from the silver maple branches that held the building in their embrace. Behind the house lay several piles of mounded dirt, freshly dug out of the snow and mud, as long as a person was tall.

The Lady slowed her steps to follow my gaze. "So you see the harm this town's children have done to our people. Do not let that trouble you. This is not the first human town we have destroyed and it shall not be the last, though it's the first whose destruction I left in my granddaughter's hands. She will deal with the escaped fire speaker soon enough, and I have no intention of letting *you* stray so far from my sight."

It took a moment to remember that the fire speaker was Ethan. "He might already be dead." The thought should have worried me, but it didn't. "He took too much fire into himself, after he came to my town."

"Truly? We shall all see him soon enough, then." The Lady drew me away from the graves to lead me down a crumbling stone staircase. We entered a basement thick with maple roots that reached down from the ceiling and pushed through the cracked concrete walls. "Cozy, is it not?" She led me to a small cave among the roots. "Almost like home."

Roots caught in my hair. Dimly I remembered that there ought not be anything cozy about a tree or its roots, but I wasn't sure why.

"You are a pleasant surprise, Liza." The Lady traced a vein along the back of my hand, and I trembled at the touch. "The first summoner we've found among humans, and Tara's daughter besides. The wolf is merely a toy, but you, Liza—you are a weapon. What was the name of your town?"

"Franklin Falls." Had I told her before?

The Lady's smile was cold as ice. "Soon we will test the extent of your power, Liza, and then you will show me the way to your mother and your town. But first we must wait for the others. Until my granddaughter and my wolf return with their prey, I think it best if you sleep." She brought her fingers to my eyelids, closing them. Velvet darkness surrounded me, and I suddenly wanted nothing more than to sleep. I curled up among the dead tree roots. It was cold there, but I wouldn't trouble the Lady with complaining. I could handle the cold.

"I very much look forward to seeing your mother again," the Lady said, and then sleep overtook me.

✌ *Chapter 9* ✌

I woke once, to the sound of Matthew's bark. When I opened my eyes, the Lady stood among the tangled roots with her hands on Johnny's shoulders, whispering fierce words. His shirt was torn, and there was blood on one arm, along with what looked like a wolf's teeth marks. My gaze went to the knife that hung sheathed at his belt. My knife. I didn't want Johnny to have it. I stood and reached for it, but then the Lady looked at me. "It displeases me to see you awake, Liza."

I didn't want to displease her. I slept once more.

I dreamed I walked through a dead forest. Ash fell like snow around me, and smoke drifted through the air, stinging my eyes, clogging my throat. I was looking for something. First I thought it was a leaf, only it was winter, and the trees had no leaves. Then I thought it was my knife, but that made no sense, because I never went anywhere without my knife.

A wolf loped toward me, its powerful gait swiftly closing the distance between us. The wolf leaped, throwing me to the ground. As I looked into his wild gray eyes, I knew that this was what I'd lost, after all. *"Matthew."* Too late I realized I'd put a command into his name. The wolf lunged at my call, gleaming teeth piercing my exposed neck—

I woke screaming, my hands grasping my throat. Someone grabbed my arm. *"Go away!"* I cried. I opened my eyes to see the Lady gazing down at me, her silver eyes bright. *"Go away!"* Beside her Matthew stiffened, ears alert, fur bristling.

The Lady laughed at my words. "You do not know my name, Summoner, but I know yours. You need not be afraid, Liza."

I heard her, didn't hear. The nightmare was with me still, making my heart pound and my breath come in gasps.

"Rest, Liza." The Lady's velvet words couldn't get past that fear. Not yet—but already my heart was beginning to slow its pounding.

I pulled my arm free, bolted to my feet, and raced past the Lady and Matthew, past where Johnny thrashed in nightmares of his own. I stumbled over tree roots, and out the door and up the stairs, into the frosty morning air. My feet kicked up powdery new snow as I ran. Clayburn's ruined buildings were to my right; beyond the trees to my left, water trickled hollowly beneath the frozen river. Thick clouds hid the sun.

As my mind cleared, I ran harder, holding my fear close, urging it to protect me. I couldn't let the Lady steal my will and my thoughts again.

She followed, calling after me in a cold chiming voice, commanding me to slow my steps. I kept running, but it was harder now, as if the air itself were thickening around me. I heard a bark—Matthew chased me, too. I almost turned back, but giving myself blindly over to the Lady wouldn't save him. I had to save myself before I could save anyone else.

Teeth bit through my pants and ankle, drawing blood. I skidded to a stop and kicked backward. My heel connected with Matthew's fur, and my leg came free. Gasping, I grabbed a branch from the ground and spun around. A weapon—I didn't want to use it.

Matthew snarled. He didn't know me. He really didn't. *"Run away, Matthew!"* My voice tightened around the words. *"Run far, far away!"*

The wolf whined. For a moment his gaze focused on me—saw me. Then he spun away and ran, crashing through snow and underbrush as he disappeared into the forest.

"And now you have made me angry." I hadn't heard the Lady run after me, but she must have, because she closed the distance between us in a few swift steps and grabbed my arm. The branch slipped from my fingers. *"Go away."* Even I could tell how feeble the words sounded.

"You must be punished for making me so angry." The words sank down deep, making my bones ache. How could I not accept whatever punishment she deemed just? "What shall I turn you into? A fish, perhaps, abandoned to strangle on dry land? Or a tree, left to die alongside all the other trees as this world slowly winds down?"

I said nothing, knowing I would accept whatever she demanded, knowing I never should have run. A last echo of fear shuddered through me and was gone.

"And yet, I have need of you." The Lady's hair was down, but glimmering light seemed to cling to it still. "A deer, perhaps—but deer are skittish things. Horses are skittish, too, but they submit to the bridle well enough." Her grip tightened around my arm, and I felt power ripple through me—

The Lady's hand fell abruptly away. I remained human, which puzzled me. The Lady drew a single sharp breath, she who made so little sound. Her gaze was on something beyond me. I turned, hoping my few steps wouldn't anger her further.

Someone walked toward us through the trees. A faerie woman, in old denim pants and a leather jacket, wearing a small backpack. Her hair was pulled into a long, clear braid that fell over one shoulder. I hadn't heard her steps any more than I'd heard the Lady, or Elin.

"Karin?" My thoughts were muddled and slow. What was Caleb's sister doing here? A bone-handled knife was sheathed in her boot, and a bracelet of green ivy circled her wrist, its leaves oddly bright in this world of bare trees and gray sky.

Karin nodded at me, then dropped to one knee before the Lady. "Mother," she said. "It has been a long time."

Karin was the Lady's daughter? There was something odd about that, too. I moved closer to the Lady, reaching for her arm. She ignored me. For long moments neither she nor Karin spoke. I could have run then, only I no longer remembered why I'd wanted to.

At last the Lady took Karin's hand and lifted her to her feet. "I had not thought to see you alive again, daughter." Her voice held no expression.

"The years since the War have been long," Karin agreed, her voice just as flat. A brown ragweed vine poked through the snow and wrapped around her boot. "I take it you are well?"

"As well as can be expected in such fallen times. I would hear the story of your travels, and how we come to meet this day, but first I must deal with this disobedient human. I promise it will not take long." Her cold fingers grasped mine, and I knew she hadn't forgotten me.

That was good. I didn't wish to be forgotten. I wished to be a fish, or a horse, or whatever else the Lady required.

Karin brushed her braid over her shoulder, a deliberate gesture. "I come seeking my student." She tilted her head toward me. "I see you have found her, and I thank you for it."

"I see no plant speakers here, nor none of the blood, either." The Lady's voice was cool, polite.

"In these times we teach whom we must," Karin said. "Surely you no longer insist all your students be changers now?"

"Of course not. I only insist they be of the blood." An edge crept into the Lady's voice. If Karin was her daughter, didn't she know better than to anger her mother?

Light snow began to fall. My ankle ached where Matthew's teeth had dug in. I hadn't noticed before.

"Though Liza be human, her power is great," Karin said. "I value her. If she has done you any harm, I will make amends for it."

"There is surely some mistake." Sharp as hawkweed

thorns, the Lady's words. I flinched, glad those words weren't aimed at me, even as the Lady said, "Liza, my daughter claims to be your teacher. Does she speak true?"

The question was a strange one. "Faerie folk cannot lie."

The Lady's smile was a cold and glittering thing. "Yet we have been known to slant our words from time to time. Is she your teacher?"

I had no teachers. Mom had taught all the other children in my town, but no one had taught me, not until this winter.

Except for Karin. What little I knew of magic—that visions were less terrible when spoken aloud, that magic could save as well as destroy—I'd learned from her. My own mother had suggested it might be best if I continue to learn from her.

I did not want to leave the Lady's side, but neither could I lie. "She has taught me, yes."

The Lady's face darkened, the way storm clouds did when they blocked the sun. "Very well, Daughter. Take her, then."

Karin's gaze didn't waver. "Release your hold on her first. She is under my protection, as all students are under the protection of their teachers."

"You presume much." The Lady released my hand and brushed her fingers lightly over my arm. Something left me, and I fell to my knees, understanding at last how small and weak I truly was. The Lady smiled, and I flinched from the daggers in her gaze, knowing they could cut right through me. She was still beautiful, though, beautiful as a new-sharpened blade.

Karin drew me to my feet. There was anger in her silver eyes, and a hint of the Lady's perfect beauty as well. I fought the urge to bow before her, too, as if something of glamour lingered in me yet. My head dipped, just a little, and Karin lifted it.

"Not to me, Liza." She whispered the words close to my ear, so low I doubted even the Lady could hear. "Never to me."

I looked at her, knew her. She was Karin, only Karin. For some reason the thought brought tears to my eyes, and I was too weak to fight them.

"It is good to see you well, Daughter." Only the faintest echo of storm-cloud anger lingered on the Lady's face. "I look forward to learning more of the events that have brought you here this day. Will you and your"— she paused meaningfully—"*student* join me for a glass of wine? A few pre-Iron bottles yet remain, and I have brought one with me."

"I truly regret that I cannot join you." Karin bowed her head. "But my student and I have much to discuss. I am sure you understand."

"Oh, I understand." How had I ever found the Lady's voice anything but threatening? "You will do as you must. As shall I. I am certain we will meet again. In the meantime, I have some matters of my own to tend to. Did you know, Daughter, that Tara yet lives?"

"I have heard something of it." If Karin had any reaction to the words, I couldn't hear it in her voice.

The Lady had said she meant to go after Mom. I shivered as snowflakes landed in my hair, melted, and trickled down my neck. How could I have forgotten?

I couldn't do anything for Mom if I remained here under the Lady's power, any more than I could help Matthew or Kyle or—

Johnny. "There's a boy from my town here."

The Lady raised her pale eyebrows. "Is that one your student too, Daughter?"

Karin looked down, and the ragweed vine unwound from around her boot to retreat into the snow. "No."

We couldn't leave him. I had to make Karin understand.

She nodded at her mother, a respectful gesture. "Root and Branch and all Powers go with you."

"And with you." There was no warmth in the Lady's voice.

Karin turned from her mother, and she walked away. Just like that. For a moment I didn't move, as if glamour held me still. The Lady gave me a long, disdainful look. "Go on, then. Follow your teacher."

I hurried after Karin, catching up with her where the path left the town. My footsteps creaked against the damp snow; hers made no sound. "We can't leave him there."

"I have no intention of it." Karin didn't slow her pace. "But first I must get you to safety. We will think on what to do after that."

I didn't slow down, either, but I told myself I'd return for Johnny, one way or another. No one deserved to be left helpless under the Lady's power. At least I'd gotten Matthew free, and maybe Kyle as well. Kyle had run in the same direction we now walked. *He couldn't possibly outrun a hawk.* "I'll come back." I spoke the words aloud, making them a promise.

The path turned to follow the frozen river. We picked our way downstream along its uneven bank. Snow landed on my cheeks and bare hands. "You came for me." My voice seemed loud in the chill air. I lowered it, though there was no sign the Lady had followed us. "I called you, and you came."

"It is not the first time." Karin smiled, as if it were a small thing.

It was not a small thing. "That's twice you've saved me."

Karin frowned, and the green leaves around her wrist stirred restlessly. "I would not declare either of us saved yet. The Lady is a powerful enemy, and she'll not soon forget the insults we've exchanged this day."

She'd done worse than insult me. "I won't forget, either." I reached for my knife and remembered that the Lady had it. Until I'd met her, I'd had no idea how helpless I truly was.

Panic shuddered through me, and once I started shaking, I couldn't stop. I thought of the Lady's fingers brushing my hand, my hair, of how I'd smiled as she'd talked about killing my mother, of how I'd slept at her command. I would have done anything she asked of me— anything. Even now it would take but a word from her, and I'd be nothing more than a weapon in her hands once more. I stumbled, nearly fell.

Karin's hand caught my shoulder, steadying me. "Liza." She took my face in her hands, making me meet her eyes. "You are safe for now. You must believe that."

Safety was an illusion. I'd always known it. Matthew had, too. I thought of how he'd snarled at me, how he'd flopped down at the Lady's feet. "Nothing's safe." Even my voice shook. He'd forgotten me, for no other reason than that the Lady wished him to.

Karin's gaze hardened, and I saw anger once more. She wrapped her arms around me, her posture more protective than comforting. "I am so very sorry for all she has done to you." There was steel in Karin's words, and for the first time, I almost believed she had fought in the War. "You have my word that I will do all I can to shield you from her."

She didn't promise that it would be enough. I wouldn't have believed her if she had. I managed to still my shaking. "I will do what I can not to need protecting."

"I know that." Karin nodded respectfully as she drew away. "I watched you set off to rescue your mother, though you had little chance of success. I heard of how you brought her out of dying Faerie, and brought my brother back from beyond death as well, at no small risk to yourself. You need not convince me, Liza, of your strength or your will to face hardship. I'll do what I can just the same."

The snow grew steadier as we started walking again, away from Clayburn and my town both, toward Karin and Caleb's town. I wanted to stop, to turn around—I couldn't bring myself to take a single step back toward the Lady. I hadn't thought myself a coward before.

A length of brown kudzu broke through the snow, reached for Karin, then sighed and fell still. "Understand, Liza, that my people take the bond between teacher and student quite seriously, as seriously as that between parent and child. The Lady is no more free to directly interfere with that bond than anyone else. This gains us some time, if nothing else."

I reached once more for the knife I didn't have. "Who *is* she?"

Snow landed in Karin's clear hair and froze there. "My mother has gone by many names—the Lady of Air and Darkness, the Ruler of the Realm, the Queen of Faerie."

I hadn't known that Faerie had a queen. Even Before, my town had been ruled by the Council. The Council had been ruled by a governor, the governor by a congress and a court and a president. There were queens in the old stories, though. "She's truly your mother?"

"She truly is." There was sorrow in Karin's voice.

That made Caleb the Lady's son. *The children of powerful people, Liza, nothing more.* But it didn't tell me who Mom was, or what role she and Caleb had played in the War. Cold bit my fingers and the tips of my ears. My hat and gloves were still in my pockets, along with the dried meat. I tugged the hat down over my ears, pulled my gloves up beneath my ruined sweater sleeves.

I tore a strip of meat in half and offered some to Karin. She took it and chewed slowly. I bit into my half more fiercely. The taste of smoked goat steadied me. My scarf remained around my neck, looser now. The ends were still bound together, as if they'd been crafted that way.

Karin reached out to trace her finger along the wool. "Weaver work?" she asked.

Snow blurred the bluffs and the forest. "That's what Elin called it."

Karin stopped abruptly and took the scarf in her hand. "Elin." She spoke the name slowly, as if it were strange on her tongue.

"That's not her true name." If it had been, I'd have gotten Johnny and Kyle well away before the Lady knew of any of us.

"No, it is not." Karin's voice was soft.

"The Lady sent Elin after Kyle," I said. "As a hawk. She told her to kill him, and Elin swore she would. She's nearly as terrible as the Lady."

Karin shut her eyes a moment, as if my words were arrows that had found their mark. "I think you'd best tell me all that has happened since you left your town." She started walking again.

So did I, though I knew that the more distance we put between us and the Lady, the longer it would take to return. I wasn't sure I could face her again—I had no choice. Caleb might be in Karin's town, and Caleb could help Ethan—but Ethan might well have died of his burns by now. Johnny was still alive, and perhaps Kyle as well.

There was still time to save them. "Karin, we have to go back."

"If it were up to me," Karin said, "I would tell you to stay safe behind my town's Wall while I deal with this, for all that the Wall sleeps this winter, and so provides less protection than before."

"It isn't up to you?" Karin's footprints were lighter than mine, snow already filling them in. I'd be easier for the Lady to track than she would, if it came down to that.

Karin looked into the falling snow. "Your decisions are your own. I'll not force them on you."

Snow landed on my scarf, my gloves. I remembered how in my vision Karin had offered to bind my mother when Caleb had refused. I hadn't understood what her words meant then. "You could force decisions on me. Couldn't you?"

"I will not, though more than our own lives be at stake. You are safe with me, Liza. Do you understand?"

Faerie folk cannot lie. Something relaxed in me, a fear I hadn't been aware of. "I understand." I held my shoulders a little less tightly as I told Karin all that had happened, starting with Johnny, and Kyle, and the burned children who'd died of Ethan's magic—at Elin's command.

When I told Karin about the leaf, she stopped me, wanting to know, as the Lady had, how I'd come by it.

"Oak and ash," Karin whispered when I told her that Mom had given it to me, and that Caleb had given it to Mom. "Kaylen, you *are* a fool." She pronounced Caleb's true name differently than Mom did, weaving a sound like wind through leaves into it.

I lifted an ash branch from the ground, discarded it, and picked up a longer branch. As a weapon it wasn't much, but it felt better to have something in my hand. "His foolishness may have saved Kyle's life."

"I know." Karin stroked the leaves around her wrist, as if drawing comfort from them. We veered toward the river, following a narrow track between the trees and the frozen water. I used the branch as a staff, taking some of the weight from my ankle, though already the pain there was fading.

Something green poked through the snow, bright against the whiteness. *Spring,* I thought, but it wasn't a plant. I reached down and took a faded plastic frog in my hand. My fingers tightened around it. I remembered a row of plastic frogs, lined up at the edge of a tub.

Karin tilted her head, a question.

"Kyle's been here." For the first time since meeting the Lady's eyes, I felt something other than gray despair. "He made it this far."

～ *Chapter 10* ～

The ice near the river's shore was cracked, as if Kyle had run over it so swiftly it hadn't—quite—given way beneath his weight. I listened to the water trickling beneath it. If that ice was almost too thin for a five-year-old, it would be far too thin for me. I slipped the frog into my pocket and followed the river downstream, seeking a better crossing.

Karin touched my arm and pointed upward. A hawk circled above the bluffs—Elin? Did that mean Kyle was nearby, too? Or did it mean we were already too late?

The ice remained thin, but—there. A row of rocks jutted out of the half-frozen water. I followed the stepping stones across, careful of my balance on the slick rocks. Karin followed more gracefully, as if ice were a small matter to her. On the other side she leaned down and shoved her hands into the snow. Yellow Bermuda grass pushed through it to wrap around her arms. Karin closed her eyes, listening to something I couldn't hear. "He passed this way," she said.

The grasses sighed wearily and retreated back into the snow. "They're not dead," I said. "Not completely, not around you."

"They are not dead." Karin sounded as tired as the grasses had. "But they are dying. Tell me, Liza, do you believe that spring will come?"

Why ask me? I was no plant mage. "The adults in my town believe it." They believed in spite of the gray trees and the gray skies, the failed crops and the too-long winter.

"So it is with the human adults in my town as well." Karin held a hand out to the falling snow as we walked on. Snowflakes melted against her skin. "Yet I have never heard the trees so quiet. They yearn for darkness, and some have given way to it. Others slip into sleep, accepting that they may never wake. I am told this is the way of your world. It is not the way of mine. I have never known a forest that was not green. What do you believe?"

On the far side of the river, the bare trees were shadows through the snow. *Nothing more can grow out of such death. And so the worlds wind down, and tragedy runs its course.* "Does it matter what I believe?" If the world was winding down, it would do so no matter what I believed. A scrap of cloth lay on the ground ahead of me. Kyle's bloodstained bandage. I picked it up. Did I dare believe he might be all right? If I couldn't believe in spring, could I believe that much?

"Even if you had not called me, Liza, I'd have sought you out soon enough. What thin hope I have for spring is bound up as much in your magic as in my own." Karin took the bandage in her hands and ran her fingers over the torn weaving, as if she could mend it. "And so I am reminded once more that those things that are going to happen will happen, though we cannot always see the path." She laughed softly to herself; at what, I didn't know. "But there will be time to discuss this later."

I wrapped the bandage around my staff as we moved closer to the bluffs, picking our way among rocks to find a narrow track near the base of those cliffs. The snow was letting up. I saw a faint streak of blood against the white limestone, and another, higher up. Kyle had climbed these stones.

A winged shadow flew over us. I crouched, staff in hand, tensed to fight.

The hawk didn't attack. She landed on an outcrop above us and glared down at Karin and me. I backed away, eyes on her sharp talons, gauging whether it'd be better to fight or to run.

Karin stepped forward, though. "Elianna." She pronounced the name as strangely as she had Kaylen's. "It
has been many years, but surely you know me." Karin
held out her arm.

The hawk screeched and lifted her wings. There was
blood on her talons—Kyle's blood. Anger chased my fear
away. I moved to Karin's side as the hawk tilted her head.

I was suddenly aware of what a very pretty bird she
was. I reached for her sharp beak.

"No!" Karin stepped between us. "Liza is my student
and under my protection."

The hawk's yellow eyes flashed silver in the light. All
at once she wasn't pretty—she was deadly. She screamed
and flew at Karin, talons outstretched.

I had her name now. *"Elianna!"* I didn't call her to
me. I called her to herself, as once I'd called Matthew
from wolf back to boy.

The bird shimmered with light, feathers melting,
talons drawing back into skin—it was a faerie girl who
knocked Karin to the ground. Karin grabbed Elin's
shoulders, pulling the girl to her feet as she stood. Snow
landed on Elin's bare skin and in her tangled hair. She
lashed out at Karin's face, as if expecting talons at the
ends of her hands.

Karin grabbed those hands in her own. "Elianna."

"I do not know you." So fierce, Elin's voice. Karin

flinched. I clutched my staff, alert for any movement, any attempt by Elin to do either of us harm. Karin released Elin's hands, removed her pack, and drew a wool blanket from within. The girl pulled it around her shoulders, but the anger didn't leave her eyes. Silver light flowed over gray wool, and the blanket shaped itself into a rough dress, frayed at the hem and the sleeves.

Elin hardly seemed to notice. Her gaze was entirely on Karin. "I do not know who you are, or how you have come to wear my mother's face. I know only this: Karinna the Fierce would never consent to teach any human. My mother died fighting the human Uprising. She died bravely and well, and I'll not have you insulting her memory."

Mother? Karin was Elin's *mother*? Elin was the Lady's granddaughter; it only made sense—but Elin looked too young to have lived Before.

Faerie folk lived longer than humans. I *knew* that.

"I did not think to see you again, either." How did Karin hold her voice so steady? "I do not blame you for being angry with me. We have much to discuss."

"No. I don't believe we do." Elin stalked past us toward the river, head held high, feet bare. I thought Karin would run after her, but she only watched her go.

Snow blew into my face. "I could call her back."

Karin shook her head. "She makes her choices freely

as well. I'll not decide them for her." She closed her eyes and rested her head on her hands, and I felt as if I were witnessing something terribly private.

I silently kept guard as Elin followed the river upstream, away from us. At last Karin looked up once more. "Come. Let us find Kyle." She tied her pack closed and pulled it onto her shoulders. "I fear there will be some climbing involved."

I set my staff down, put my gloves back in my pockets, and started to climb. Karin scanned the cliffs, then began climbing beside me. The icy stone was slippery beneath my fingers, and snow stung my face. Kyle's blood streaked the most obvious handholds. How long ago had he climbed? He'd have climbed more slowly than Karin and I. It should have been easy for Elin to knock him from these cliffs.

She should have caught up with him well before the cliffs. How had Kyle gotten so far?

From above, I heard a faint singsong voice. "The ants go marching seventy hundred by seventy hundred . . ."

I climbed faster. Karin and I were higher than the trees now. Karin made her way onto a narrow ledge, and I followed, inching sideways, listening. "The ants go marching seventy-one hundred by seventy-one hundred . . ."

A foot or so above the ledge, there was a narrow hole

in the rock, too small for an adult to fit through. Karin stopped and peered into the dark. "Kyle?"

The singing stopped. *"Go away!"* Kyle cried.

Of course he wouldn't trust a stranger, not now. Karin must have realized that, too, because she moved farther along the ledge, and I moved to the opening. "Kyle?"

Silence. My fingers felt numb against the rock. Then, "Liza?"

"It's all right, Kyle. You can come out now."

I heard cloth scraping stone. Kyle's boots emerged from the hole, and his legs scrambled down to the ledge as he grasped the rocks. Talons had torn the back of his coat, and blood seeped through. He clung to the stone as he turned to look at me, eyes wide, quia leaf still hanging from his neck. "Scared," he whispered.

"I know," I said. "Ready to climb down?"

Kyle nodded solemnly. He followed me along the ledge, and then we descended together. His scabbed-over hand began bleeding again, but he seemed to have full use of it. We jumped the last few inches to the ground. Kyle looked up at me, lower lip quivering. He was going to be all right.

He burst into sobs and threw himself at me.

My arms stiffened around him. For a wild moment I didn't know what to do. I stroked his tangled hair, as

Mom had mine when I was little. Such a small thing—it hadn't seemed small when Mom had done it.

Karin jumped to the ground beside us. Kyle's sobs turned to shivers as he drew away from me. Karin nodded solemnly. "It is good to see you well, Kyle."

"Kyle, this is Karin. She—"

Kyle turned his back on her. His small body trembled. "I'm hungry," he said.

I offered him some dried meat, but he shook his head. Tears streaked his face. "Not hungry for *that*." He sat down in the snow.

I put the jerky back into my pocket; I had nothing else to offer him. This was no time to be a picky eater.

The snow fell harder. "We need to get him somewhere warm," I told Karin. "Maybe we can find shelter among the cliffs." A larger cave, nearer to the ground.

Karin nodded. The clouds were thick and dark, the day more than half done. I put my gloves back on. "Ready to walk?" I asked Kyle. His bleeding hand was already scabbing over again.

He crossed his arms over his chest. "No."

"We have to walk, Kyle. There's no other way. I'm sorry."

Kyle looked up defiantly. "Carry me."

Carrying him would slow us down. I was tired and my ankle hurt and I didn't feel much like walking myself—I drew a deep breath. "Would piggyback do?"

Kyle sniffed and nodded. I bent down, and he climbed onto my back, wrapping his arms and legs around me so tightly they hurt. I grabbed my stick from the ground for balance as I stood and started walking, Karin by my side.

I glanced back just in time to see Kyle stick his tongue out at her.

"Kyle!" I gave Karin an apologetic look as he buried his head against my shoulder.

"It is all right. He has little reason to trust me, and reason enough for fear, given what he's seen of my people." Karin smiled sadly. "Fear can be a sort of protection, too. Allow him to trust his instincts. He'll work this out for himself, given time. As, I believe, did you."

I looked away, ashamed of how little I'd trusted her and Caleb when we'd first met.

"She's mean," Kyle whispered into my hair.

Karin laughed at that, a lighter sound. "I am a teacher. I'm accustomed to being told I am mean."

The wind picked up. I rubbed Kyle's bare hands with my gloved ones. He sniffled, and snot dripped down into my scarf. The snow took on an icy edge. I saw gaps among the stones, but none were large enough to shelter us.

Karin pointed ahead. I squinted—there. A dull sheen of metal in the distance. As we drew closer, I saw that it was an old truck from Before. The truck's nose was half-buried in the dirt, past the front wheels, as if the earth had tried to swallow it whole during the War. The trailer was still good, though, the rust beneath the faded orange and white paint only beginning to break through the metal.

Kyle clung to me as Karin and I pushed the trailer door up. It creaked, and the oily old-car smell that made me think of Before wafted out. There were no wild animals living inside, just an empty metal shell about as tall as I was. A torn-up couch stood against one wall, its cushions gone. A few small, rusted cans were piled in one corner, and the words on them were from Before, too: *Pepsi, Coca-Cola, Red Bull.* A hole in one corner of the ceiling let the cold in, and bird droppings streaked the wall beneath it.

I carried Kyle inside, and Karin closed the door behind us. "When you can, Liza, we need to look at his back."

I nodded. Like all raptors since the War, hawks had poison in their talons. At least, real hawks did; I didn't know about a hawk that had started as a girl. I got Kyle onto the couch. He crawled into my lap, clinging still. Karin drew a pair of stones from her pack, the smaller of which glowed with orange light. She tapped the small stone against the larger one, and the larger one began to glow as well. Kyle's eyes widened. He reached for the light, then pulled away and gave Karin a suspicious look. Karin set the larger stone down on the arm of the couch. Its light was warm, taking the edge off the cold around us. We wouldn't have to waste time coaxing a fire from wet wood. Karin lit a second stone the same way. I remembered that there was a child in her town who could bring light to stones, too.

I unbuttoned Kyle's coat. "Let's take this off."

"No."

"Please, Kyle."

Kyle bit his lip and looked up at me. "Will it hurt?"

"It might." I couldn't lie to him. I didn't want to—I'd always hated when adults said that things wouldn't hurt when they would. I searched for words that would help him, thought of the time Mom had pulled a dozen dandelion thorns from my arm, one by one. "You'll have to be very brave," I told Kyle, remembering what Mom had said then. Her words had surprised me; more often Mom told me it was okay not to be brave, but the thorns had had to come out. "Can you do that, Kyle?"

He gave me a suspicious look, then nodded. Mom had given me some of Jayce's whisky before she'd begun work, but I didn't tell Kyle that. He winced as I eased off his jacket and the clotted blood beneath it tore away. "You *are* brave," I said.

There was more blood on his sweater—Kyle screamed

when I pulled it and his undershirt off. He fled my arms to huddle in a corner.

I followed him. "I'm sorry. But you have to let me look at your back. It will hurt worse later if you don't."

"Hurts worse now," Kyle whimpered.

"I know." I reached out my hand, and he took it. Somehow I got him back to the couch and lying on his stomach. His back was a mess of puffy red gashes and dried blood. Even if there was no poison, the wounds were clearly infected.

"Cold," he muttered as I stroked his hair.

His skin didn't feel cold. It felt fever hot. Karin moved, frowning, to my side. "Kaylen would make quick work of such injuries." She handed me a water skin from her pack. "Clean it as best you can. I'm no healer, but I know something of the healing that plants can do. I'll see what I can find."

Karin raised the door and slid outside, taking her pack with her. The world beyond the trailer had become a blur of blowing white. Was Matthew out in that storm, or had he found shelter, too? I wished he were here. We were supposed to be together for all the hard things. The door creaked as Karin pulled it shut behind her. I hoped Matthew had run far, far from Clayburn and the Lady's reach. Maybe he'd gone to get Caleb and help for Ethan after all.

Kyle sat up. Caleb's quia leaf dangled against his bare chest. I took the frog from my pocket and handed it to him. Kyle grabbed the toy and lifted his head proudly. "I left it on purpose, so you and Johnny could find me." His face scrunched into a frown. "Where's Johnny?"

I swallowed hard.

"Find him." Kyle stumbled to his feet.

I grabbed his arm. "Later. First you have to get well, then we have to wait for the snow to stop. Then we'll look for Johnny."

Kyle clutched the frog close. "Promise?"

"Promise. But you have to let me get you cleaned up so you can heal, all right?"

Kyle didn't fight me as I drew him back to the couch. I tore strips from my ruined sweater sleeves and wet them to clean his back as well as I could. Kyle cried and kicked the couch, but he didn't try to get up again.

"Sorry," I said, over and over, but I couldn't tell whether he heard. I washed his scabbed-over palm as well, and cut Elin's wool bandage to wrap it around his hand.

By the time I was through, I wasn't sure whether to wish I had healing magic or to be grateful I didn't. How did Caleb and Allie find it in them to treat pain, time and again, without falling apart utterly?

When Karin returned, her hair and shoulders dusted

with snow, I had Kyle wrapped in my coat and sitting up. Tears leaked out the corners of his eyes, more quietly now. "Johnny later," he whispered to the frog.

The leaves around Karin's wrist had curled in on themselves, as if against the cold. She drew dead plants from her pack, all familiar: willow bark for fever, birch bark and brown moss for drawing the infection out. If gathered while green, mosses could burn skin instead of healing it, but there was little risk of that this winter. The grasping branches of willows held dangers, too, but I suspected that Karin could manage those in any season. Plants listened when Karin spoke to them, in a deeper way than the simple calling or pushing away of my own magic.

I got Kyle out of my coat and lying down again so that Karin could pack the moss into place. He clutched his frog so tightly his fingers turned white, whether because Karin's touch hurt or because he was still scared of her, I couldn't tell. Karin laid birch bark over the moss and used bandages from her pack to tie it all in place. I helped her pull Kyle's bloodied sweater on backwards over the bandages.

Karin ground the willow bark between a couple of rocks she'd brought in with the plants. I rummaged through the cans, found a Pepsi one without rust, and poured water through the small opening. A sweet scent wafted out, like a memory of spring. Karin sprinkled the ground bark into the liquid. "The stones aren't hot enough to boil water," she said. "He'll have to drink it cold."

Kyle gave me a skeptical look when I handed him the can, and curled in on himself. I couldn't blame him; few small children accepted willow bark without fuss. "You drink it," he said.

I didn't like willow bark any more than Kyle, even now. "How about if I go first?" I brought the can to my lips and took a swallow, then immediately regretted it. Willow bark tea was bad enough—I scrunched my face with the effort not to spit the cold bitter liquid up again.

Kyle burst out laughing. "Silly Liza!"

I held the can out to him as bitterness flowed down my throat. "Your turn." Kyle grabbed the can and took a large gulp. He began coughing, spitting up liquid, but at least some of the medicine seemed to make it down his throat.

Karin pulled something else out of her bag: a thin silver blanket that crinkled like plastic as she wrapped it around Kyle. He stopped coughing to grab a handful of the strangely metallic fabric.

"The material is warmer than it appears, though I do not fully understand why," Karin said. "It was crafted by your people, not mine." She got Kyle lying on his side and drew the quia leaf from his neck. Kyle didn't seem to notice. He kept crinkling the blanket, more sleepily now.

"I doubt Tara even knew what my brother gave her." Karin handed the leaf to me. "He told me he lost it during the War. I suppose in a sense he did. Keep it safe, Liza."

I'd rather Kyle wore it, but the concern in Karin's eyes stopped me from saying so. *It will protect you in dark forests.* "What is it?" Why was the Lady so eager to get it back?

Karin tucked one of the warm stones beneath Kyle's blanket. "It is . . . a piece of our souls, you might say, though that is a human way of phrasing it. Better to say a piece of who we are lies in Faerie, bound into the First Tree, and this is the token of it. The leaf provides some protection, but carries some risk as well, for to harm the leaf is to harm its owner."

The silver felt warm in my hand. "Caleb's life is tied to this?"

"Indeed. He must have cared for your mother more deeply than I understood, to entrust her with it. I never trusted any of my consorts so, not through many long years."

Yet Karin had parted with her leaf, too. It was in the Wall that protected her town—I'd seen that in my visions. How had the woman who'd once spoken so easily of binding humans become someone who'd risk her life and soul to protect a human town?

I slipped Caleb's chain over my head and tucked the leaf beneath my sweater. Would I part with it again, knowing that Caleb's life was linked to it? I sat beside Kyle on the edge of the couch. Kyle let go of the blanket and grabbed my hand. "Stay," he said.

Beyond the small hole in the ceiling, blowing snow hid the sky. "I'm not going anywhere." I pulled on my coat and rolled onto the couch beside Kyle. He snuggled up against me, blanket crinkling.

"Look after him," Karin said softly. "I will listen and keep watch."

"I can help," I said. "Just as soon as—"

Karin touched my shoulder. "You are helping. Hold to your task, and I will hold to mine."

I wrapped my arms around Kyle, warming him, wondering how he could trust me so readily. "You know what?" I whispered to him.

"What?" Kyle's voice was sleepy and slow.

"You're not just brave. You're also a fast runner, to escape from that hawk."

Kyle giggled. "Not fast, Liza. I'm too little to run fast. But I'm a good yeller. I *yelled* the bird away!"

Before I could ask what he meant by that, he was asleep.

⌇ *Chapter 11* ⌇

Kyle slept in fits and starts. I woke when he did, so slept in short snatches, never long enough to dream. Sometimes Kyle woke screaming, sometimes crying. Once he called Johnny's name, telling him over and over that he was sorry about the ants. Another time he muttered, "No, no, no, no, no," until he drifted off again. I held him, told him he was safe for now, and thought about all the ways I'd make Elin suffer for this if I ever saw her again.

Eventually the light outside faded. Much later, Kyle's fever broke and he fell into a deeper sleep. I brushed his sweaty hair from his forehead. My chest felt strange and tight. I'd known Kyle all his life, but I'd never thought much about him before. Now I felt as if I'd do anything to protect him. That scared me—I knew well enough how little I could do to keep him safe.

When I felt myself slipping into deeper sleep, I gently pulled away from Kyle and stood, my head brushing the trailer's rusty ceiling. I didn't want to wake him with one of my nightmares.

Karin sat cross-legged by the door, the other orange stone beside her—its light was lasting a lot longer than the ones from Seth's little sister did. Karin had unbuttoned her jacket, and I glimpsed another knife sheathed inside. She'd not carried any weapons I could see when last we'd met, but the trees had been awake then, and she'd had the entire forest at her command. Her shoulders were stiff, her expression watchful. I heard a faint pattering against the roof. Ice.

"I fear we will be here some time." Karin offered me her water skin as I sat beside her. I drank, grateful for the cold water against my dry lips and throat.

"Kyle isn't ready to travel yet anyway." My stomach was grumbling again. I drew a strip of jerky—the meat Kyle had refused—from my pocket and split it with Karin. She offered me a handful of dried fruit in turn. "Blueberries," she said at my puzzled look.

That was what I'd thought; I wouldn't have hesitated otherwise. The berries should have burned my skin, but apparently they were quite dead. I set one hesitantly on my tongue, and tart sweetness flooded my mouth. Karin was the only person I knew who could harvest fruit safely. I stowed the rest of the berries in my coat pocket, though I could easily have eaten them all. Maybe Kyle would like them better than dried meat. "Karin, do you think the Lady is looking for us?"

"The storm that stops us will stop her as well, for a time," Karin said.

"What about after the storm?" I kept my voice low so as not to wake Kyle.

Karin stared into the dimness. "No. I don't think she'll look for us. I think she'll look for your mother."

I very much look forward to seeing your mother again. Karin's glowing stone couldn't keep away all the cold.

"Liza, could you get Kyle to my town by yourself?"

I shook my head. I could, but I wouldn't. I knew why Karin was asking, but I'd not abandon Mom to the Lady, not while my thoughts were my own. My hand went to the chain around my neck. I wasn't sure I'd ever be able to bring myself to part with its protection again.

Karin sighed, and the leaves around her wrist fluttered restlessly. "I am willing enough to face my mother alone, and I cannot deny I would feel more at ease knowing you and Kyle were far away from her. She is almost certainly relying on your concern for your mother. She knows we'll follow her to your town, and she has time enough to make plans against us that even the bond between student and teacher cannot shield you from. It may be that the best way to thwart those plans is for you and Kyle not to appear."

Ice tapped more loudly against the metal ceiling. "Karin, why does the Lady hate my mother so?"

Karin turned to me. "Tara did not tell you? When she returned?"

"She hardly told me *anything*." I hated how my voice sounded, like a whining child who couldn't get her way.

"You don't want this story from me, Liza." By the orange light Karin's face looked less pale—more human. "The storm will not last forever, and we have other matters to discuss."

The ice didn't sound as if it were letting up anytime soon. "How long was Mom glamoured for?" I shivered in my coat. I understood now why Mom didn't want to speak of glamour. I didn't want to speak of it, either. "How long did Caleb—" I stopped abruptly, afraid Karin wouldn't want to hear me speak badly of him.

"I do not know." Karin lifted a stray screw from the floor and rolled it between her fingers. Its threads were thin and precise, as only work from Before was. "I paid little attention, in those days, to the games my brother and his companions played with humans. I ought to have paid more attention. If I had, I might have seen sooner what was happening between Kaylen and Tara, but I was more concerned with trying to be what my mother needed than with protecting my youngest brother."

I didn't need to ask if she thought she'd succeeded in pleasing the Lady. I heard it in her voice. "I was never who my father wanted, either," I said. My voice sounded too loud in the small space.

"Yet you stood up to him at the last." Karin carefully set the screw down on the floor. It rolled away just the same. "Kaylen told me."

I looked down, ashamed. "I didn't send him away soon enough." Caleb must have told her that, too.

"None of us can change what we've already done, Liza." Karin's hand brushed my shoulder. I flinched, and she drew respectfully away. "That the past cannot be un-done was one of the War's hardest lessons. We remain responsible for our actions there, but we have no power over them. We only have power over the thing we do next."

"Even under glamour? Are we responsible then?" I traced a finger through the dust on the floor. Dust from Before—it smelled of oil, too. "Karin, how often did you—" I stopped myself. Karin had fought in the War. No doubt she'd used glamour in ways I could scarcely imagine, and other weapons as well.

"Never as a game." Karin stared at the orange light between us. "And never since the War. Kaylen understood, sooner than me, that your people are not mere toys. I did not understand until I heard their cries as they died. I did not understand until I came to a human town, and began to care for its people, and they for me. I understand now."

Why should it take death to understand such a thing? Yet I hadn't understood until a few months ago that Karin's people weren't all monsters, either. "Karin, Mom says you think she and Caleb started the War. Do you?" *Did they?*

Karin laughed, but there was no joy in it. "Tara always did have a way of simplifying things. Fault and blame are complicated matters. Tara and Kaylen played a role, certainly. So did I, and my mother, and Tara's father."

The children of powerful people, nothing more. "Who was Mom's father?" I'd never known any of my grandparents.

"Who people are is never simple in your world," Karin said. "Among your people, position is not defined by birth or strength of magic. Tara's father was neither a wielder of power nor a maker of goods—he was merely a merchant, a procurer and seller of the goods others made, weapons in particular. In my world, such a person would be of little consequence. I did not understand how different matters were in your world until your mother—" Karin stopped abruptly. "I cannot tell this fairly, Liza."

"I'd rather hear it unfairly than not at all." *Mom had her chance to tell me fairly.*

"I know less than you think." The vine around Karin's wrist unwound a little, creeping toward her fingers. "I did not note when your mother first found her way into Faerie. I do not know how she and Kaylen came to care for one another, even through the glamour my people use so easily upon yours that we do not even think of it as part of our magic. I don't know what made Kaylen certain the caring was more than a part of the illusions he wove. My brother did not ask my advice in those days, and if he had, he would not have liked the advice I'd have given. I know only that Kaylen lifted the glamour from Tara at the last and, in doing so, swore an oath to never use glamour against your people again. I have since taken the same oath, though I was slower to do so."

"You thought he was reckless to make promises to humans," I said.

Karin looked sharply up, and I remembered I only knew that from my vision. "If I thought Kaylen reckless for releasing your mother," she said in a level voice, "I had some cause, given what Tara did next. Once her thoughts were her own, once she understood what had happened to her, she grew wild with anger and fear, like the child she was. She fled from Kaylen, back to her human home."

I'd seen that, too. Wind blew ice pellets against the trailer walls. I shuddered, remembering how the Lady had bent my very thoughts to her desires. "Of course Mom ran." How could Karin have expected her to do otherwise?

"You do not understand. Tara told her father everything. She gave no thought to who he was. She thought only of her own pain. Yet she found no comfort in the telling, and so she fled her father as well. She returned to Kaylen, seeking—I don't know what she sought. Love? Protection? A means of forgetting her pain? You'll have to ask her, for I truly do not know. I know only that her father followed after her, and that much grief resulted from that in the end."

"The War resulted from it." My words were nearly lost to the noise of ice and wind. "But Mom couldn't have known what would happen. She wouldn't have gone back, if she had."

"We all would do differently, could the seers read the consequences of our actions more clearly. That doesn't make us any less responsible for those actions, no matter how much we wish it otherwise."

Wind gusted through the hole in the ceiling. Mom

had to tell someone what had happened. She hadn't been wrong about that. Maybe her father hadn't been like mine. Maybe she hadn't known he was the wrong person to tell. "It wasn't her fault. Not all of it."

"Nor did I say it was." Karin gazed at the ivy around her fingers. "I know well enough Tara did not move my hands and my voice when I commanded the trees to attack your people. I'm responsible for my actions, too. And so I save those I can, where I can, and will continue to do so as long as I draw breath. Can Tara say as much?"

"Mom's saved people, too. In my town." How many more would have fallen to magic, like Jayce's granddaughter, if not for Mom?

"I know. Kaylen told me." There was no forgiveness in Karin's tone. She brushed her hand over the vine, and it retreated to wrap back around her wrist.

I wasn't sure I forgave Mom, either. She hadn't saved me, after all. Why was it so much easier to hate Mom for her failures, when Mom had never wanted the War to happen, than to hate Karin, who had attacked my people of her own will once it had? "Karin, why did you fight in the War?"

Karin was silent so long I thought she'd decided not to answer. Kyle stirred in his sleep, throwing off the blanket. I got up to wrap it back around him. He muttered something about mean ants and fell back asleep. I put my hand to his forehead. His skin was cool. Which mattered more—the people we saved or those we failed to save? I thought of Ethan, surely dead or near to it by now. I thought of Johnny, still with the Lady. I rubbed my wrist. The skin beneath Matthew's hair tie was red where my sweater had tightened around it.

"I fought in the War because I believed it necessary to protect my people." So quiet, Karin's voice behind me. "And I fought because I wanted to please my mother."

Kyle had flung his frog from the couch. I picked it up. How could anyone fight a war to please someone else? I squeezed the soft plastic in my hand. Once I might have killed for my father if he'd asked it, too. I tucked the frog in beside Kyle and returned to Karin's side, drawing my arms around my knees. "Were things simpler Before?"

Karin laid a hand on my shoulder, and this time, I let her. "Few things were ever simple, in your world or in mine."

Kyle sighed in his sleep. Karin shut her eyes, though her posture remained watchful. "My mother alone would not have acted differently had the seers told her what was to come. The Lady was known for many things, but forgiveness was not among them. The memories of my people run long. My mother will not rest until she finishes the work the War began."

The Realm will be avenged before this is through, and

your frail human towns will fall, one by one. "She won't stop until we're all dead."

"I will do all I can to stop her." Karin's voice was grim. "Do not doubt it."

I looked right at her. "So will I." The words sounded foolish as I spoke them. What could I possibly do against glamour? Even if I held Caleb's leaf close, that wouldn't protect anyone but me.

"There remains a part of me that wishes you would return to my town and be safe." Karin pressed an ivy leaf between her fingers. "And there is the part of me that knows too much is at stake to refuse your help. Even so, I'll not have you face the Lady again without your consent. This began long before you were born. It is not your battle."

She was wrong about that. "The Lady has threatened my town, and my mother, and my—and Matthew. She has threatened all that I hold dear." I was proud of how my voice held steady. "It doesn't matter how this began. It is my battle, and I will not run from it."

Karin looked away from my gaze. "It is hard, sometimes, to believe you are Tara's daughter." She shook her head, as if regretting the words. "I welcome your help on this journey."

"I'll save who I can, as I can, too. I promise, Karin, no matter how—"

"Careful, Liza. Words have power, for faerie folk and humans with magic alike. Even words spoken lightly may shape your actions later."

There was nothing light about the words I spoke. "I will do all I can to protect my people and my town."

Karin gave me a measuring look. Father had looked at me that way sometimes, and had always found me wanting. Karin smiled, though. "Very well. I'll give you what tools I can before we leave this place. Tell me what you've learned of magic since we last met."

I started with the shadows I'd learned to lay to rest this winter, but she had me go back further, to the first shadow I'd called, before I knew my power for what it was. The ice grew quieter. I huddled down in my jacket as I told Karin of my other callings as well, those that had succeeded and those that had failed. I told her of my struggles to control my visions.

"That much is no failure on your part, though it may feel like one," Karin said. "Visions always begin untamed and unpredictable, and trying to fight them only makes it worse. As useful as a seer who could look willfully into the future might be right now, it will be some time before you have such power."

"Mom said I needed to learn to control my visions." I'd struggled with that.

Karin shook her head. "For a seer, control comes

only with time. In the meanwhile, it is best to focus on your summoning. Indeed, it is your summoning that would have led me to seek you out even had you not called for my help. Tell me about how you called the quia tree again, Liza."

I told her all I could remember about calling the tree—how I'd brought a seed home from the same gray land I'd called Caleb back from after he'd nearly died saving Mom; how the green within that seed had given me the strength to leave that lifeless place; how I'd tried to call the green from the seed into my world in turn, and how I'd called the reds and oranges of autumn into it instead. "Was I wrong to call the quia tree? Or is this just the way winter was Before?"

My hands were trembling. Karin took them in hers, stilling them. "I don't know. I have spent many hours trying to make sense of the pathways by which your people say leaves fell from the trees Before. Their understanding differs from mine. I was taught that human plants have always looked to the Realm to remind them, in spring, how to grow, and so are but a faint echo of that which is real. Who can say which understanding runs closer to the truth? What I do know is this: what thread of life remains in the Realm is thin. There is little for human plants to look to, if they have lost their memory of greenness and of life."

Wind tapped at the trailer door, as if trying to get in. "So it may be my fault the world is winding down after all."

"I would not go so far as to say this world winds down." Karin drew a winged maple seed from her pocket. "Take it."

I held it by the stem, wary of the fire maple seeds held, but it was cold, as all seeds were this winter. "It's dead."

"Is it?" Karin smiled, a little sadly. "Look closer."

I stared at the seed as hard as I could, but I saw only brown. I closed my eyes and reached for it with my magic, just as I had with so many seeds this winter, but nothing reached back. "They're all dead." I fought to keep the despair from my voice.

Karin took the glowing orange stone in her hand. It cast its light onto the seed, giving it a faint tint that reminded me of autumn. The color wasn't real, though. Only the brown within the seed was real.

"Look at the shadow," Karin said.

The orange light cast a faint maple seed shadow onto the floor. I stared at that, but it was an ordinary shadow, no more alive than the shadows cast by sun and candles. Karin moved the light directly overhead, and the shadow disappeared.

I looked at her, not understanding, not wanting to admit I didn't understand.

Karin nodded, as if I'd done nothing unexpected. "Keep trying." She moved the light about. I watched as the shadow shifted on the floor, as it disappeared, reappeared, and disappeared again. Outside, trees creaked as the wind blew through them, but I didn't look away from that moving patch of darkness, seeing again and again the moment when it disappeared entirely.

My eyes grew weary. I blinked, trying to keep my focus. For just a moment, the shadow seemed to cling to the seed before it disappeared. I forced my eyes to stay firmly open the next time, but I didn't see it again.

I softened my focus instead. There—a hint of inky darkness, clinging to the seed. The shadow cast by Karin's light shifted about, but the darker shadow held fast to the seed, so close—so much a part of the seed— that I wasn't sure how I saw it at all. I drew the seed nearer to my face. I wasn't imagining it.

Karin set her stone down beside her. I squinted to see in the dimness. The seed's shadow held even without light.

"So you see," Karin said. "All things that live and grow have shadows, from the smallest seed to your people and mine."

I looked at Karin, keeping my focus soft. I looked at Kyle, tangled in his blanket. I looked at my own hands. I saw no shadows there.

Karin brushed a strand of hair from her face. "We can work on human shadows later, if you like. Those will be harder, for my magic is only with plants, much as Kyle's is only with animals. I cannot see human or faerie shadows, though I can guide you toward them. Only a summoner can perceive the shadows in all things—and if the price of greater strength is lesser subtlety, well, it's strength we're going to need to call back spring."

"I can't call anything back. I keep trying, and I always fail." I let the seed slip from my fingers. It twirled toward the floor, shadow clinging to it still.

Karin caught it in her cupped hands. "Try again, only this time, call to the shadow, not the seed."

I kept my soft sideways focus on the shadow. I felt—not growth, not life, but a sort of lingering sleepy existence that told me sleep and death were not the same thing after all.

I reached for that. *"Come here,"* I whispered.

The seed shuddered in Karin's hands. A pale white root shot out from it, and a brown stem followed. Something arced between me and the seed, a thin thread shivering with the faint will to grow. Two brown leaves pushed through the seed coat—and then with a sigh the small plant fell limp, and the thread dissolved to shadowy dust. The dust drifted off, leaving no shadow clinging to the dead plant Karin held.

I sighed. "I'm sorry."

Karin laughed at that. "Liza, those two leaves are more than I've been able to call all winter." She let the seed fall from her hands and touched the vine around her wrist. "My power is much diminished, in this season of dying trees. Even the leaves I wear cling to life only because I did not allow them to slip into sleep when autumn came, and because I speak to them of growing often enough that they do not have the chance to forget it. It is a great deal of work. My magic is with living plants, not with shadows that hover at the edge of death. I cannot call back a sleeping forest, but what you've just done tells me that, just maybe, you can, if we find a way to hold the life you call into this world once it begins to grow—and if you are willing to try, for it is not without risk."

Outside, the wind was dying, but in the trailer I shivered. If this gray winter was my fault—if it was—this might be my one chance to make it right. It seemed too much to hope for. "Of course I'm willing."

Karin let out a breath, as if she'd doubted it. "We need not act right away. It may be that spring will yet find its own way back into this world, as your people expect, heeding the call of light and warmth and requiring neither summoning nor the memories of the Realm to help it return. We have time yet to summon spring. More time than we have to stop my mother."

My thoughts spun back to the Lady. "We should go." I glanced at Kyle. He slept soundly, and I didn't look forward to waking him. I didn't look forward to carrying him through the wind and the dark, either. He needed rest, but the ice had stopped and the wind was letting up, which meant the Lady could set out for my town anytime.

"Tell me of the other children in your town," Karin said. "If we can find any the Lady's glamour has not touched when we get there, will you speak with them? Can we rely on their help?"

Afters stick together. "They'll help us."

"All right, then. I can teach you little more of magic, in so short a time, that will make you any more effective against the Lady. But I can at least give you this much: I can take your oath before we leave."

I stared at the vine that nuzzled Karin's wrist like an affectionate cat. I'd heard Karin give the oath before, in her town, to a child who had just come into his magic. The words had angered me then, with their easy promises to do no harm with magic. They made me uneasy now. "I'm not sure I can."

Karin's eyes narrowed, and the leaves around her wrist went still. "Do the words trouble you, Liza?"

I met her level gaze. "No one can promise not to do harm with magic, least of all me." I already *had* done harm with my magic: to Ethan, and perhaps to Mom as well. Magic was merely a weapon, no worse than the one who wielded it—but weapons slipped in the hand, arrows went astray, blades were blunter or sharper than expected, the wielder proved too weak for the task. "And if the Lady gets hold of me again—" I drew an unsteady breath. "Anything could happen then."

Karin looked at me thoughtfully. "I think perhaps you do not understand what the oath is for."

"Tell me, then." There was a challenge in my words.

"Very well." Karin rested her chin on her hands. "The oath cannot protect against the error in judgment, the failure of knowledge, or the lack of skill. Avoiding harm is not so simple as flipping the switch linked to a human generator, knowing that light will always follow. What the oath demands is that you always choose with care, with the intent of not doing harm—and that when you cause harm in spite of these efforts, you do all you can to mend it. The oath may also provide some small protection against those who would sway your thoughts toward harm, but that has never been tested."

"Wait—the oath is *protection*?"

Karin stroked her ivy leaves, and one by one they curled up. "It is no promise of safety, only of mindfulness. Yet mindfulness is a sort of protection, too."

"There are no promises of safety," I said.

"Even before the War, this was true. Will you give me your oath?"

I nodded slowly, knowing that once I spoke the words, I had to mean them. "All right."

I thought of the child who'd taken the oath in Karin's town, surrounded by family and townsfolk who'd known him all his life. Here there were only Karin and I, the soft creaking of wind through trees, and the softer sound of Kyle's breathing. Karin spoke, her voice quiet and sure, and I repeated after her:

> *Blessed are the powers that grant me magic.*
> *I promise to use their gift well.*
> *To help mend my world,*
> *To help mend all worlds.*
> *And should I forget to mend,*
> *Should I refuse to mend,*
> *Still I will remember*
> *To do no harm.*

My voice trembled at first but grew steadier as I went on. Something inside me shifted, not the terrible twisting of my thoughts I'd felt with the Lady, but the steadier feeling of having found level ground on an uneven slope. I would do all I could. I'd always done all I could and thought it was never enough.

It was enough. That was what the oath meant. I would mend where I could, fight what I could, and put everything I had into both the mending and the fighting. If I failed, it would not be for lack of courage or action.

"Thank you," I whispered.

"You are welcome, Tara's daughter." Karin squeezed my hand. "I will do all I can to be worthy of your trust."

Through the hole in the ceiling, the night wasn't quite as dark as before. It was time to go. I stood, stretching stiff legs, and walked to Kyle's side. Outside, the wind had stopped. A hawk cried out, and Kyle bolted upright on the couch, throwing his blanket aside.

"She's looking for me," he said.

~ *Chapter 12* ~

"Who's looking for you?" I asked, though I feared I knew.

"The hawk." Moss and bark fell out of Kyle's sweater. I didn't have to ask which hawk he meant.

Ice tinkled to the ground as Karin slid the trailer door open. "Wait here." She slipped outside and pulled the door shut again.

I would have followed, but that would have meant leaving Kyle alone. I took off his sweater and sat beside him, picking the remaining moss from beneath his bandages and rewrapping the bandages over his wounds, which were a less angry shade of red, the puffiness around them gone. He'd lost the bandage around his hand in the night, but the scabs there were thicker now and seemed to be holding this time.

I put his sweater on again, still backward, to protect his back, and he crawled into my lap. There was no sign of fever in his eyes, and his skin remained cool. He was as ready to travel as could be hoped for. He was shaking, though, and not with cold. "Mean bird," he muttered. "Mean, mean bird."

"I won't let Elin hurt you." I was surprised I could speak the words aloud. None of our promises were a surety of safety, but magic wasn't concerned with that, only with whether we meant what we said.

I couldn't tell if Kyle had heard me. "Go 'way," he whispered under his breath. "Go 'way, stupid bird."

The oath is protection. Scant protection, perhaps, but hadn't I just vowed to do all I could? I drew Kyle close. If the oath could protect me, it could protect him, too. "Before we go, I have some words I need for you to re-peat. Can you do that?"

Kyle looked up at me. "I'm hungry."

How long had it been since he'd last eaten? I pulled the dried blueberries from my pocket and handed them to him. Kyle sniffed them skeptically, then tasted one.

A startled grin crossed his face. He grabbed the rest of the berries and shoved them all into his mouth at once. Blue stained his lips and tongue. He held out his hand. "More."

I didn't have any more. I handed him a strip of jerky

instead. Kyle gave me a suspicious look but took the meat and ate it, too. Karin's water skin was in the trailer, beside her pack. Kyle drank deeply when I handed it to him. Then he looked up at me.

"I want you to repeat what I say, Kyle, okay?" I waited until Kyle nodded, and then I spoke the oath, one line at a time.

Kyle bit his lip and repeated the words, his expression growing serious as he did. He added a couple of things at the end: a promise to try not to be mean, another promise not to send ants into his brother's pants ever again. Only then did he nod at me, as if satisfied.

I tore the last of my jerky in half and handed Kyle the larger piece. He chewed it solemnly. The door creaked open, and Karin stepped inside, her jacket wrapped around a bundle in her arms.

I nudged Kyle from my lap to put myself between him and what Karin held. She crouched down, set the bundle on the floor, and unwrapped the shivering creature she held, a red-tailed hawk who stared at us through baleful yellow eyes. Elin—I watched warily as Karin looked her over. Feathers had been torn from her left wing, and blood streaked both it and her chest. Hawks were day creatures. Elin would have been at a disadvantage if she'd met other wild animals at night.

The hawk lifted her head and screeched. The sound

echoed through the trailer as she swiveled her head to fix her gaze on Kyle.

"I don't have it, stupid bird!" Kyle scrambled to his feet on the couch behind me even as Karin grabbed Elin in the jacket once more.

Pursue the animal speaker. Destroy him, and bring the leaf he bears back to me. Do not return until you have it. The Lady had changed Elin and sent her out again. She must have. "*I* have the leaf," I told her. If she wanted to fight someone for it, she could fight me.

The hawk shivered in Karin's arms. "Liza, can you hand me the stones?"

I didn't move. "Elin made Ethan burn his own people. She thought it was some sort of test."

"My mother's tests are harsh indeed." Karin looked troubled, and I remembered that she'd talked of passing the Lady's tests in my visions, too.

Being troubled wouldn't protect Kyle or me if Elin decided to attack. "She can't stay with us."

Holding the bird awkwardly with one arm, Karin knelt to pick up the nearer orange stone herself. She looked up at me, asking me to understand—understand what?

"You can't ask this of me." I remembered how Kyle smiled as his hand grew slick with the blood that Elin had demanded to see. "Of us."

"I ask only that you not interfere." Karin tucked the stone into the jacket. Elin made a soft meeping sound as her shivering eased. Had she been out in the storm looking for Kyle all night? Surely no one, hawk or human, could survive so long in the ice and the cold.

Elin wasn't human. Fey folk were harder to hurt—and harder to heal—than humans were. "She can't be trusted." Behind me I felt Kyle clutching my coat.

"No," Karin agreed. She gave me a searching look. "I ask much of you by even bringing her here. I know that, and I take full responsibility for it. Yet I cannot leave her." Her voice dropped. "I have left her too often before."

The trailer door remained open. Beyond it, the black sky was giving way to gray. Soon the sun would rise. We needed to leave this place. "If she turns her glamour and her magic on us, or forces us to turn our magic on ourselves? What then?"

"She hardly has the strength to—" Karin stopped mid-sentence. When she spoke again, her voice was cold. "If she harms either of you in any way, I will see to stopping her myself, though it mean her life. You have my word."

Elin gave a strangled squawk. She struggled in Karin's arms, pushing free of the jacket, and tried to launch into the air. Her injured wing failed her, and instead she landed on the trailer floor. She lifted her head to glare at Kyle and me.

"She says she doesn't understand why you put humans ahead of your own people," Kyle whispered. "She says you should kill us all. She says—no!" Kyle pushed past me and ran at Elin. *"Go away!"* he screamed. *"Away 'way 'way!"*

I grabbed Kyle. He fought me, but I didn't let go. I wouldn't let Elin hurt him.

Elin wasn't trying to hurt him, though. She was backing away, talons scraping metal, left wing dragging.

Kyle wriggled out of my arms. *"Go away, stupid bird!"* He clenched his small fists and advanced on Elin. She backed into the corner and hunkered down there, trembling.

I yelled the bird away. I drew a soft breath. Karin's eyes widened, and I knew she'd figured it out as well.

A slow smile crossed my face. Kyle wasn't helpless after all.

Elin looked up at him, her yellow eyes fierce. Kyle's hands went slack. His steps grew slow and dreamlike. "Pretty bird?" He sounded uncertain.

I grabbed him. Karin grabbed Elin. "They're *both* under my protection," she hissed at the bird.

Elin squawked her protest. Kyle went rigid in my arms, the glamour's brief hold on him lost. *"Go away!"*

Elin fought her mother again, though there was nowhere left to go. A talon tore Karin's sweater, drawing blood, but she scarcely seemed to notice.

"That's enough, Kyle," I said. I didn't want Elin hurting Karin, and it was clear enough Karin wasn't going to let her daughter go.

Kyle stuck out his tongue at the hawk. "*Told* you I could yell her away."

I thought of how he'd asked—no, *told*—the ants to leave the Store. I squeezed him tightly before I set him down. "Good job, Kyle."

Elin stopped fighting and trembled in Karin's arms. Karin stroked the hawk's feathers. "It is not unknown for animal speaking to move beyond ordinary speech into commands—it is much like plant speaking that way—though usually command comes when the speaker is older."

Kyle glared at Elin as he leaned against me. "He didn't even need her name," I said.

"It is only people who require names. Animals and plants do not use them. Still, to be able to speak to the animal even in one who has been changed or shifted—one who has a name when in another form—takes considerable power. Kyle is in a fair amount of danger."

I drew him close. "He's in less danger, if he has that much power."

"He's also of more interest to those who would use that power for their own purposes."

Like the Lady. Had she wanted Kyle killed because he was useless—or because she feared anyone who might be able to control those she transformed? It was hard to believe that the Lady feared anything.

Karin set Elin down again, found her water skin, and stashed it in her pack. "I should have Kyle's oath before we go," she said.

Kyle helped me fold the blanket, but his gaze kept straying to Elin. I was glad. The warier he was, the better. "I already took his oath."

Karin blinked. "You intend to teach him, then?"

"The oath isn't about teaching." *Is it?*

"The oath is about many things." Karin took the blanket, put it in the pack, and tied the pack closed. Kyle hung behind me, clutching the edge of my coat with one hand and his frog with the other. I was responsible for him. That was what the oath meant.

I got Kyle's hands into the sleeves of his coat and buttoned it up. I traced the bloodied slashes along the coat's back and glanced at Elin. At least with his sweater on backward, no part of him was fully exposed to the cold.

I hesitated, then took my leather gloves and set them beside Karin's pack. She'd need protection if she intended to carry the hawk. I turned away before she could thank me, still wishing she'd leave Elin behind.

I tied my knife belt around my waist, though the sheath was empty. "Ready?" I asked Kyle. I couldn't do anything about his gloveless hands, but I wrapped my scarf around his neck. The woven-together ends would help keep it in place, and I wouldn't let Elin anywhere near the wool.

Kyle held his head up high. "Now we find Johnny, right?"

"Right." I climbed outside. The ground was slick with ice, and I grabbed the trailer for balance. Cold metal stung my palms. I cursed and jerked away. The clouds were gone, and through the trees I saw an orange glow at the horizon. I reached for Kyle and helped him out. He slipped, and I caught his hand, steadying him. Karin climbed out after him, green ivy hidden beneath gloves that met her jacket sleeves and hawk balanced on one leather-clad fist. She didn't stumble as she landed silently on the ice.

The sun poked above the horizon, breaking through the trees. Light hit the branches around us, turning them bright as broken glass. The light hurt my eyes. I blinked hard against it, and as I did I saw—

Kyle, crying. Johnny holding him and whispering, "Hey, kid, don't worry what she says. I'll take care of you." "Promise?" Kyle sniffled. "Promise," Johnny said—

The Lady, glowering down at Elin while ice fell around them both. "I told you not to return without the leaf. Why do you continue to disobey me?" Elin held up her hands, as if to explain, but the Lady grasped her wrist. In moments she was a red-tailed hawk once more, launching into the dark. Behind her the Lady whispered, "And so Kaylen will pay for his foolishness with the human girl at last—"

The Lady, marching through an ice-sheathed forest that glittered in the early-morning sun. Johnny marched by her side, a gray wolf at his heels—

"Liza." Karin's quiet voice drew me out of my visions as gently as Mom's voice drew me out of nightmares. I opened my eyes to the shining trees around me. Kyle still held my hand.

"She found Matthew." Had the Lady gone looking for him, or had he returned on his own, looking for Johnny and me? It didn't matter. "We have to find them." Matthew and I were supposed to keep each other safe. What was the point of whatever was between us if we couldn't do that much?

"You are certain it was not the future you saw?" Karin asked. Elin hunkered down on her fist, talons digging into leather, as if she would deny us all.

"I don't think so." Though there was no wind, the

dawn was cold. "It was morning, and there was ice on the trees."

"Best not to let any more time pass, then." Karin looked at me. "Ice and sun will present challenges for you as a seer. Do your best not to focus on any one spot for too long—but do not try so hard that you are not careful of your footing. Kyle, if Liza stops walking, can you squeeze her hand? That will help wake her out of visions."

Kyle nodded soberly. "Can I pinch her, too?"

A smile pulled at Karin's lips. "If you wish."

I kept a wary eye on Elin as we set out. Ice coated the limestone bluffs, the white snow, the path we walked. My steps were maddeningly slow over the slick ice. I wished *I* were a hawk, not bound to the slippery earth. My thoughts kept turning to Matthew, imagining the Lady's fingers running through his fur, imagining Matthew trotting behind her, obeying her every command.

The glimmering ice tugged at my gaze, like a child eager to show all her toys. Fragments of vision flickered at the edges of my sight.

Elin, running through underground tunnels, younger, alone—

The Lady, her hands on Elin's shoulders. "How dare you let your control of the firestarter slip? You will find him. You will destroy him and all the escaped children who have caused our people grief with their magic this day—"

Matthew, running along a snow-covered path, running so hard his paws bled—

We crossed the river, Kyle and I making our way slowly over slick rocks, and even Karin choosing her steps with care. I'd hoped to cut through the forest and so gain some time, but the ground was too slippery. We followed the path toward Clayburn.

Elin watching Clayburn's houses burn, her hand on Ethan's arm—

Elin turning away from the sound of screaming, the sight of bright flames licking wood. Elin kneeling to throw up in the snow—

Ethan shuddering as if just coming awake, then creeping away from Elin's side—

The sun rose higher, turning the sky a deep blue. "Stop," Kyle whispered.

I stopped. "Why?"

Kyle pinched my arm. "That's why!"

"Hey!"

Kyle giggled. Karin laughed, too. Elin twisted her head to glower at us. Karin shifted the hawk from one fist to the other as we walked on.

Darkness flickered within the ice-sheathed trees.

Shadows—the trees hadn't lost their shadows with the coming of winter after all, any more than the seeds had. They'd merely drawn that last bit of darkness close, as if to hold it safe. I softened my gaze, focusing on the shadows instead of the ice, and the visions came less often.

Hope calling up wind, her hands raised high, her face grim. Only then her hands fell slack, and she smiled—

Mom, standing on Kate's back porch, looking into the Lady's cold eyes. "Do to me as you will. I will fear you no longer—"

It was hard not to walk too fast over the treacherous ice.

As we neared Clayburn, Karin paused beside something silver that shone against the ground. Elin's butterfly, feebly flapping its wings. "You kept it," Karin whispered as she took the butterfly in one hand. She raised the hawk toward her, but Elin turned away.

"Set it free." Kyle lifted his chin toward the butterfly. A faint shadow clung to its metal wings.

"If I set it free, it will die." Karin frowned as she straightened a bent wing tip.

Better to die than to remain helpless, trapped in silver forever. "Where did Elin get such an awful thing?"

"It was a gift." Karin sighed. "From her mother." She fastened the clip into her own hair, above her braid.

In Clayburn ice sheathed the burned houses, sheathed,

too, the burned bodies around them. Kyle dug his finger-
nails into my hand. Karin's steps grew slower, more
deliberate—there was anger there. On her shoulder, Elin
craned her hawk's head this way and that, as if so much
death were a matter of mere curiosity, as if those deaths
weren't all her fault.

"She says they smell bad," Kyle whispered.

Karin stroked Elin's feathers. "I know," she whispered, though the smell was faint now, decay slowed by
the cold and the ice.

I held Kyle's hand firmly as we turned onto the
path away from Clayburn. Tracks broke through the ice:
a human foot, a wolf's paw. Trees creaked around us.
Even if spring came, some trees would die beneath this
winter ice.

A younger Elin with tears streaming down her
cheeks. "Why won't you allow me to go with you? I do
not lack the courage—"

Karin, lips pressed firmly together. "You are too
young for this battle, Elianna. I will protect you a time
longer, if I can. There is a chance you might survive this
War, while I know that I will not—"

Kyle pinched my arm, harder this time. I slipped and
fell butt-first onto the ice. Kyle laughed. Karin reached
out a hand. I looked up at her as I took it and struggled to
my feet. She'd left her daughter, too, left her because of

the War, but stayed away to teach human children. I glanced at the hawk on her fist, but Elin's head was hidden beneath one wing. The other hung awkwardly by her side.

The air grew warmer as the sun edged past noon. Light glinted off a water droplet that hung, half-frozen, from a branch.

Matthew—eyes bright, soot-streaked hair falling into his face—saying, "I'll go faster alone—"

I focused on setting my feet down on the ice and making sure I didn't fall again.

Too soon we came to shards of white bone poking through the snow. The ashes of the dead children gave a sickly-gray cast to the ice that covered their remains.

Elin made a strange, strangled sound I'd never heard any bird make. "She's crying," Kyle whispered.

Crying wouldn't bring them back. Elin was responsible for the things she did, too.

We found my pack among the ashes, coated with ice. I pulled out the dried meat within and shared it with the others. Someone—the Lady?—had severed my bowstring. I hesitated—Father had helped me make that bow, and it could be restrung back home—then left it and the pack where they lay. They'd only weigh me down.

"Tired," Kyle muttered as we left ash and bone behind. The snow turned to slush, and we walked faster.

Through the trees I caught glimpses of the wider road that would lead us back to my town. I rubbed the leather around my wrist. Soon we would be home. What would we find when we got there?

Something at the meeting of the path and the road caught the light, something slick and liquid. I slowed my steps, squinting for a better look. Karin moved to my side as I realized what lay there.

No. "Get back, Kyle." I didn't want him to see this.

I forced myself to keep moving forward. The afternoon sun seemed distant and cold. *I* didn't want to see this.

Johnny lay on his back, hands clasped around the knife—my knife—that was plunged through his heart. A smile was frozen on his face, and he'd clearly been dead for some time.

∽ *Chapter 13* ∾

Blood spread like a bright red flower from the wound, glinting in the sun. More blood stained Johnny's wrists and his throat.

Kyle howled and threw himself at his brother. Elin screeched and flapped from Karin's shoulder, her injured wing, with its torn feathers, straining. She missed the branch she aimed for, landing on a lower one instead. Karin scarcely seemed to notice. Her face held no expression as she knelt and thrust her hands into a clump of mud and brown grass.

I ran to Kyle's side. He was shaking Johnny as hard as his small hands could. "Wake up," he said. "Wake up, wake up, wake up!"

"*Johnny!*" I called, but I knew I was too late to bring him back. "*Jonathan!*" I couldn't look away from the smile on his lips. He'd been glad to do what the Lady wanted, even as he'd died.

Kyle stopped shaking his brother and looked at me. "Sleeping?" he asked.

I couldn't lie. I knew it beyond doubting now, because I wanted to so badly. "Not sleeping." My throat hurt.

Kyle's lip quivered. He couldn't lie, either, couldn't deny what was true—it was too much. I knelt and reached for him, and he threw himself at me, fists raised. He punched my chest, again and again, with surprising force for such a small child. I let him. I could handle this, could handle it better than the way Johnny's eyes stared at the sky.

Kyle's howls turned to shuddering sobs. I drew him closer, remaining alert for anyone whose approach might mean us harm, all the while knowing I wouldn't hear the Lady if she chose to attack. I couldn't do anything about that, so I did what I could: held Kyle until he cried himself out.

At last he fell hiccuping against me. I rubbed his back and looked over his head at Karin. She drew her hands back from the dying plants. "They passed this way sometime before noon."

We were too late. Anger burned in me. Elin sat on her branch, watching us through unblinking eyes. This was her fault. She'd led us to the Lady. If not for her, Johnny would be alive.

"*Elianna!*" I drew away from Kyle and scrambled to my feet. "*Elianna, come here!*" Elin trembled on her branch. I didn't call her out of the hawk this time. I only called her to me.

She fluttered down to my arm, her injured wing forcing her to take a jagged path. I glared into her yellow hawk's eyes. She glared back, matching hate with hate, but she didn't leave my arm. She couldn't. I felt my command, cold and glimmering between us.

"Liza." Karin stepped toward us.

Right here, right now, I could be rid of Elin. I might have been powerless with the Lady, but I wasn't powerless now. I could command Elin to go so far away she would never wake again.

The trees creaked softly. Elin's talons tightened around my jacket. If I let go my control, even for a moment, she could shatter bone with those claws. "Tell me why I shouldn't do this."

"You must decide for yourself what needs doing." Karin held her hands out in front of her. "I tell you only this: there is a difference between acting out of anger and acting out of need. Which is this, Liza?"

Kyle held Johnny's bloodstained hand, whispering words too low to hear. Who would dare take chances with this magic that controlled actions and thoughts? How could we not go to War against such power?

"It is all right to be angry." Karin had stopped moving toward me. "It is all right to be frightened."

"So long as you don't let your fear show." I repeated Father's old lesson automatically.

"No. So long as you don't let your fear control you." Karin looked toward Elin, then me. She held out her fist.

I looked into the hawk's eyes. Did she know fear, too? "I'll still kill her if there's need. I won't hesitate."

"I know," Karin said.

My arm trembled as I whispered, *"Go, Elianna."* She half hopped, half flew from my arm to Karin's glove.

Karin kept looking at me. "Save your blame for the one who most deserves it. My mother often tired of her human toys and sent them to horrible fates, but this is something more. With this death she tells us to turn back, knowing full well we will not heed her warning. That's part of her game."

"Is that all human lives are to your people?" Anger was with me still, in my every word. "A game?"

"Your people played no games, that is true." I couldn't read Karin's expression. "They were always in earnest, from the moment they asked to meet with us. Perhaps they wept when their fire fell from Faerie skies.

Perhaps they did not laugh as my people did. Their tears saved no lives."

I looked to Kyle, who clutched his brother's hand in silence now. "We have to stop her."

"Oh, yes." Karin's voice was cold as falling ice. "I am through playing my mother's games. She will be stopped, no matter the cost. You have my word."

"Good." But I took a step back, uneasy beneath her hard gaze. Just then, I didn't doubt she'd once commanded the forest to attack.

Kyle was crying again. I knelt by his side. Both footprints and paw prints turned onto the road, leading away from this place and toward my town. *The wolf is merely a toy.* How long did we have before the Lady decided Matthew's life was worth no more than Johnny's?

I laid my hand on Kyle's shoulder. "We have to go."

Kyle looked up, nose running, eyes rimmed with red. "Take him with us."

"We can't take him, Kyle."

Kyle pressed his lips together. "Carry him."

"We can't. I'm sorry." Johnny was too close to my height and weight. I couldn't carry him for long.

I thought Kyle would argue, but he only said in a small voice, "Later?"

"Later. I promise." I eased Johnny's hands from around my knife, then hesitated. Would carrying a knife put us in more danger, should the Lady use glamour against me? The power she'd have over my magic would be far more deadly if it came down to that. Until then, I would wield every weapon I could. I pulled the knife free.

It slid cleanly from Johnny's chest, as if he were no more than a deer felled on a hunt. I fought a wave of nausea as I wiped the blood from my blade in the mud. For an instant some hint of shadow seemed to cling to Johnny's cold skin. I blinked hard, and it was gone.

I sheathed the knife in my belt. Kyle took the frog from his pocket and set it carefully on Johnny's chest, over the wound. "Later," he whispered, then looked up. "Carry *me*?" His voice was forlorn, as if he knew it was too much to hope for.

I was so tired—it didn't matter. "Carry you," I agreed. I knelt so Kyle could wrap his legs around my waist and his arms around my neck. He sighed and leaned wearily on my shoulder as I stood.

Karin knelt by Johnny's side. "Powers protect you," she whispered, and it sounded like a prayer.

I focused on following footprints and paw prints through the slush, on pushing through the bleak fear that chilled me even as melting ice dripped from the branches. Kyle sniffled against my neck. *I chose,* I realized. *I chose Kyle over Matthew and Johnny both when I gave him the leaf.* I thought of how Mom had chosen the other children—and her memories of Faerie—over me, of how Karin had chosen a town full of humans over Elin. How did anyone ever choose one person over another? How did they live with those choices afterward?

Kyle shifted to look behind us, then all at once cried out, "Johnny!"

"He's gone." My throat ached. How often had I wished Johnny would just go away?

"Not gone." Kyle's voice was stubborn. "Down," he said.

"Kyle—"

"Down!" He wriggled from my back and ran toward Johnny. I turned and ran after him, past Karin and Elin.

My breath caught. A dark shadow rose from where Johnny lay. Legs, arms, and face took shape out of that darkness as Kyle ran at it. I tried to grab him; so did Karin. We were both too late. Kyle threw his arms around the darkness. He shuddered, as with cold, then drew back and reached for the shadow's hand. Shadow fingers wrapped around his. Kyle's shivering eased, and he lifted his head to look at me. "Told you, Liza."

The shadow was growing more solid, like a charcoal sketch of the boy Johnny had been. I reached for his other hand, but my fingers went right through his, and cold knifed up my arm. I jerked away. This shadow wasn't for me—it was for Kyle.

It didn't matter who Johnny's shadow was here for. I reached for his hand again, but he drew back. "I'm sorry, Johnny." I wasn't sure how I managed to speak. "But this isn't real. And I can give you rest."

The shadow shook his head. Johnny always had been stubborn.

"He promised," Kyle said.

I'll take care of you. Promise. "That was before, Kyle. He can't—"

"Not sleeping," Kyle said firmly, and squeezed his brother's hand.

I thought I'd shatter like old plastic if I spoke a single word. I began walking again, and Johnny and Kyle walked beside me.

This was so wrong. I looked to Karin as she joined us.

"I cannot tell you what to do here." Karin stroked Elin's feathers. The bird shrank from her touch. "I know no more than you what is right. I know only that the shadow appears to be doing Kyle no physical harm."

Kyle's father had shivered to death when he'd held a shadow too close. Yet I'd carried a shadow once, too, when there had been need. Kyle only held Johnny's hand now; he hadn't tried to hug his brother again. Perhaps he knew what was right better than either Karin or I. He was happily babbling to his brother: about the ice storm, about how he'd hidden in the rocks, about how I'd taken care of him in the trailer, about how he'd used his magic to keep Elin away.

I pressed on through slush that was giving way to mud. The sun was sinking, gold light reflecting off dripping ice.

Matthew watching as Johnny took my knife to his chest. His wolf's eyes showed little interest as steel pierced skin and blood bloomed around it. The Lady moved to Matthew's side, and Matthew leaned into her touch—

Matthew—a younger Matthew, who'd just turned into a wolf and back again for the first time—looking small and lost as he stood naked at the edge of our town, his skin crisscrossed with ragged cuts and his wrist punctured by blackberry thorns—

Matthew running, running away on swift paws as I called his name. His shadow trailed behind him, dissolving like dust in the sun, and I knew I'd lost him, lost him beyond recall, for all that I kept running after him—

I stumbled, caught myself, and walked faster. I'd failed him. I'd lost him. I brought my wrist to my face. Matthew's hair tie still smelled faintly of wolf. He wasn't lost yet. "Karin, are visions always true?"

Karin didn't slow her pace as she turned to me. "What have you seen?"

Karin was the one who'd taught me that visions had less power if put into words, yet I feared speaking this vision aloud would only turn it true. "Matthew's in trouble."

A dead sycamore leaf fell from a branch. Karin caught it in her free hand. "The seers did not expect me to survive the War." She stared at the leaf's brown veins. "No future is entirely fixed, though neither are visions easily or often averted."

I had to avert this. Wind began to blow, with a wet, bitter edge that cut through my jacket. I couldn't fail Matthew like I'd failed Johnny. *Not Matthew.*

The world didn't care what I needed or wanted. It knew only that some people could be saved and others couldn't, and that all we could do wasn't always enough.

Kyle kept talking to Johnny. His voice and the wind were the only sounds in the forest. Kyle bent into that wind, but Johnny didn't seem to notice it.

The road narrowed as we turned to follow the river outside my town. Snow and ice were nearly gone, and the sun dipped below the horizon, making it glow. Soon the light would be gone.

Elin shifted restlessly on Karin's glove, as if she knew that as a hawk she didn't belong out at night. Kyle fell silent at last, but he didn't let Johnny's hand go. I slowed my steps, watching for any sign of a trap that had been set for us. The trees grew thicker. A grove overflowed the forest onto the path.

That wasn't right. I knew this path. I'd followed it on hunts. There should be no trees here. I looked at the oaks and maples, willows and birches, poplars and dogwoods. Some of them were river trees, some slope trees, some trees of the forest flats. They didn't belong together.

Karin stopped, letting the sycamore leaf slip from her fingers. There was something strange about these trees' shadows. I softened my gaze, trying to see more. Karin put one hand to the bark of a brown locust tree.

The shapes of the shadows; that was what was wrong. Within each tree shadow I saw something more, something human, a rough outline of arms that pressed against wood, of legs that turned to roots and disappeared into the earth.

Karin drew a sharp breath. "Jayce?" she asked softly. She touched another tree. "And Kate. You know these names?"

A chill ran down to my sodden feet. Karin walked among the trees, whispering the names of more towns-folk. Their clothes were scattered among the dead leaves, as if they'd been carelessly discarded.

The Lady couldn't only change people into animals. She'd said as much when she'd spoken of turning me into a tree. Still, I hadn't thought—

She'd changed the townsfolk, changed them into

winter trees. The wind died and silence thickened around us. "Are they all right?"

Karin brought her hand to another tree, and another. Elin's head twisted around, watching her. "They are weary, as are all the trees in the forest," Karin said. "Like all the trees, they slowly die of winter."

"I can call them back." I let Kyle go and reached for Kate's tree, a furrowed brown sassafras.

Karin set her hand over mine, stopping me. "They have been trees for some hours now. That would not be long in a different season, but they have been listening to winter's voice all that time, and I have spoken with enough trees these past months to know how powerful a voice it is. As trees they endure, because trees die slow. As humans they might return to life—or they might die faster, remembering winter still. If we can wait for spring, it would be safer to call them out then."

Cold shivered through me. I felt a faint spark of life in Kate's shadow reaching toward me.

"Sorry," I whispered as I stepped away, not sure Kate could hear. Was Mom trapped among these trees, too? Was Matthew? No, I saw wolf prints continuing through the mud.

Kyle knelt on the ground, digging his hands into the brown leaves around a dead log, while Johnny stood watchfully behind him. I pulled Kyle to his feet. He gave me a sullen look and shoved one muddy hand into his pocket. With the other he reached for Johnny's shadow once more.

We followed Matthew's and the Lady's prints beyond the grove and into town as the sky turned to gray. The houses were silent, no windows being tacked shut, no lanterns being lit. We found more trees behind Kate's house. "Hope," Karin said. "Seth. Charlotte." Other names, of other Afters. There were scuff marks and splashes of mud around them—they'd fought the Lady before she'd overcome them. That hadn't been enough to save them. Within the trees their shadow hands pressed against the bark, as if trying to push free.

"The Afters won't be able to help us," I whispered. *The Lady changed them all.* She'd condemned them all to winter. A thick brown chestnut tree had even pushed through the roof of the shed where Ethan had been, though if any shadow remained alive within it, it was hidden by the shed's metal walls.

I lifted Charlotte's cane from the ground. The end had reshaped itself into a sharp point. I almost handed the weapon to Kyle, but he wouldn't know how to fight with it. "If anyone tries to hurt you," I told him instead, "I want you to run. You can yell animals away, but run from everyone else."

Kyle nodded seriously, tightening his grip on Johnny's shadow hand. "I'm good at running."

The light was swiftly fading. Karin took Charlotte's cane from me and set it down against an ironwood tree. "There is no time for turning back now, as my mother is no doubt aware, but all is not yet lost. Allow me to do the speaking when we meet her, but be alert for any danger, in words and actions both. If this goes badly, there is another plant speaker in my town. She is new, young and untrained, but she may be able to help you call spring."

"Goes badly how?" I demanded.

Karin didn't answer, just shifted the hawk from one fist to the other and walked on. Kyle, Johnny, and I hurried after them. "Whatever you do, Liza, do not let the Lady touch you. You too, Kyle. She can only change those she touches."

"I'll run," Kyle agreed. His face was streaked with mud.

A third set of prints joined Matthew's and the Lady's as we left Kate's house behind. Kyle began humming his ant song again, but Johnny squeezed his hand, and he fell silent. We followed the path out of town. The first stars came out, and the waning moon rose, yellow giving way to silver. We came to a familiar hillside, thick with blackberry and sumac, their thorns blurred in the dim light. In a clearing among them, a smooth-barked quia tree stretched bare branches toward the night sky.

This tree wasn't the Lady's work. It was mine. I'd called it to life and called autumn into this world with it. I didn't need to soften my gaze to see the shadow that clung to the quia's trunk and branches, sharper and clearer than any shadow I'd seen. How had I not noticed before? I'd visited this tree often enough this winter, seeking signs of life within.

Something in the quia's shadow reached for me, and the cold shimmering thread of magic between us felt familiar, as if the quia and I were old friends.

Melting ice dripped from the quia's branches. How long could we keep walking into this trap? The Lady surely knew we approached. Was she near enough to see us?

Was she near enough to *hear* us? I stopped abruptly. Maybe we didn't have to do the walking. Maybe there'd be something to gain by meeting the Lady at our call and by our choosing, rather than the other way around.

There was only one thing we needed first. I turned to Karin and asked, "What is your mother's name?"

∽ *Chapter 14* ∾

Elin screeched her anger and flew at me. I raised my arms to my face, but before I could send her away, Kyle shouted, *"Stop it, stupid bird!"* Elin squawked and wheeled off. Her injured wing strained, but this time the wing held her, and she fluttered to a low quia branch.

Karin's shoulders stiffened. She climbed the hillside to the quia tree, blackberry and sumac branches moaning as they parted before her. She looked into her daughter's eyes, but the bird turned her head away.

"I know, Elianna. I do not consider such things lightly. I never have."

"She says you can't choose humans instead of your own true people." Kyle pulled Johnny up the hillside after Karin as he spoke. I ran after them.

"She says it's bad enough you abandoned her," Kyle

said as he reached the tree. "She says you can't—" He looked up at the bird. "She can do whatever she wants." He stuck out his tongue.

"My people," Karin said as if testing the word on her tongue. "Your people." She looked at me. "It was Kaylen and Tara who first said separating our peoples made little sense. It was Kaylen who first wore his name openly among humans, though they did not understand the gift he offered them, and so insisted on shortening it. *I* did not understand, not until after the War, not until humans were born with magic." She took off my gloves to stroke the vine wrapped around her wrist. A leaf curled around her finger. "It ought not have taken magic to make me understand. Even so, my mother's name is tied up in vows that I may not lightly set aside."

She promised not to tell, I thought. "You can't speak her name, even if you want to." My voice was flat. We were going to have to walk into this trap after all.

"Oh, I can speak it. The vows I took are not so simple as that. I can speak, but if I do, I sever the bonds between myself and my people." Karin sighed; and the leaf uncurled. "In truth I severed those bonds when I entered a human town and allowed my life to become tangled with those of its people. I know why you ask this of me, Liza, and it is not badly considered. Still, I'll not try this thing until no other choices remain. There are other ways of calling." Karin set her pack down and lifted her head. "Mother! If you can hear me, come to me. Let us talk."

A breeze rippled through the forest. The Lady stepped out from among the winter trees beneath us, silent, beautiful in the growing moonlight. Even without glamour, some part of me wanted to bow at her feet. I grabbed Kyle's free hand, but he pulled away. Johnny hissed softly, the first sound I'd heard from the shadow, and moved closer to his brother's side.

The Lady ascended the hillside, two slender glasses filled with dark liquid in her hands. Her hair was once again bound in its firefly net, and her gaze fell entirely on Karin, as if the rest of us were unworthy of her notice. *Where's Matthew?*

The Lady turned her back to Kyle and me as she offered a glass to Karin. "So, Daughter. You have returned for the wine I promised. And I have returned to hear how my daughter comes to teach humans. Much has changed, in the short years since the War."

If I could drive my knife between the Lady's shoulders before she turned . . . I reached for the blade.

"I would not try that, Liza." The Lady didn't look at me. "Let your hand fall now, else the animal speaker will be under my control and gouging out his own eyes before you can draw iron."

I released the knife's hilt. Kyle edged behind the quia tree, Johnny beside him.

Karin raised her glass but did not drink. "Much has changed indeed. Truly, Mother, I did not expect to find you whiling away your time playing with humans."

The Lady shrugged, an eloquent gesture. "We all must have our entertainments." Her gaze flicked to Elin on the quia branch. "And what of you, Granddaughter? Have you brought me what I asked for? Or do you disappoint me yet again?"

The hawk made a mournful sound. The Lady extended her arm, and Elin hopped obediently down from the branch onto it. She was trembling, though, both wings drawn close to her body.

The Lady's fingers brushed her feathers. "We shall talk about your failures later." She set the hawk back on the branch and turned to me. I backed into a defensive crouch. "I believe, Daughter, that your student holds something which is mine."

Karin stepped around to put herself between us. The Lady smiled and sipped her wine. "And so you play your own games with humans, do you not?"

Karin's eyes didn't leave her mother. "I have never played at anything."

The Lady laughed. "Ah, yes. As I recall, that caused us both a fair amount of trouble at court. But I do not ask you to play today. I ask only that you return the leaf to me, as is my right."

Behind the quia tree, Kyle sang softly. Dying grasses rustled at Karin's feet. "I do not believe it is," she said. "Or have you not heard that Kaylen, too, yet lives?"

The Lady's smile was cold as starlight. "That he has not returned to the dust from which we all rose is clear enough, lest the leaf would have crumbled into that same dust. That he has long since broken every bond that ties him to the Realm is also clear, and whatever existence remains beyond that hardly matters. He chose a human over his people and his land, and the price paid for the Uprising that resulted was great. That is what happens when one ceases to play games."

Caleb had saved Mom's life. He saved lives in his town yet. But they were human lives, and no doubt beneath the Lady's notice.

She traced a finger along the rim of her half-empty glass. "I would hope, Daughter, that bonds of love and loyalty would be enough for you to do this thing. Even so, I offer you this: command your student to give me the leaf, and I will go on my way and leave you this human town to play with as you will."

My hand went to my chest. "No." Caleb's town needed him, too, and if Caleb's life was truly bound up in the leaf—I couldn't buy the lives in my town at such a price, even if spring came and I was able to call them from their trees. I couldn't save this town only to leave the Lady free to destroy other towns instead.

The Lady's fingers tightened around her glass. "Your student speaks out of turn."

Karin smiled grimly. "My student merely speaks my mind. We will not barter one life for another."

"Kaylen bartered away the lives of all our people. And so summer ends and unending winter takes hold in both the Realm and the human world. There is no plant speaker strong enough to stop this dying, just as no fire speaker could control the fires the humans sent, nor any healer stop the poison that tainted air and soil when the fires burned out. The worlds wind down, Daughter, yet justice will be done before the game is through. Give me the leaf, and let Kaylen and his human toy pay for their foolishness at last."

"No amount of justice will bring back the dead," Karin said. A breeze rattled the quia's branches. "I offer you this instead: leave the few surviving human towns alone, and take me in their stead." She dropped to both knees and emptied her glass at her mother's feet. "Punish me for Kaylen's mistakes if you wish, or demand that I return to Faerie by your side—whatever you command of me, it shall be done." Dark liquid sank into the ground as she held out her hands. *Do not let the Lady touch you.*

"No." I moved to Karin's side, meaning to say I wouldn't let her barter her life for another, either—but I couldn't say it. Karin wasn't offering herself to the Lady to save a single life or a single town, but to save my entire world. I would do the same in her place, and do it willingly.

"You disappoint me, Daughter." The Lady drained her glass, set it down in the mud, and walked past Karin, as if her offer were a trivial thing. "No matter. Justice can take many forms." She gestured toward the forest.

Mom stepped out from among the trees. I froze. Her down coat was open, and the leg of her pants was torn, as by a wolf's teeth, but otherwise she seemed unharmed. She held something in one hand—my father's knife. Matthew paced into view a step behind her, his gray wolf's eyes as dull as the skeletons of the winter trees around us.

I longed to run to them, but I didn't. There was more than one kind of trap. They were both still alive. I held to that as I tensed, waiting for a chance to act. Karin rose to her feet beside me.

"Tara, pet, come here." Mom obediently climbed the hill to the Lady's side, and Matthew paced after her. The Lady reached out a hand. Mom took it, trusting as a child. "Your mother and I have had a very interesting talk, Liza."

Ice trickled down my spine. Mom was under the Lady's glamour as surely as Matthew—the glamour she had never stopped fearing. The Lady whispered in her ear, and Mom tested the knife against her hand, not drawing blood. Her eyes were red, as if she'd been weeping, but she wasn't crying now. She waved the knife through the air as she walked toward me.

Karin's hand reached out to squeeze mine—a warning.

I pulled away to step forward. "Mom."

"Liza?" Mom's voice was fuzzy, as if she spoke through layers of wool.

"Tara, dear, remember what we discussed."

Mom's eyes focused, as if she were seeing me for the first time. She drew me, one-armed, into a hug—a child's hug, seeking comfort, not giving it. "I've missed you, Lizzy."

I drew away to reach for her knife. Mom smiled, a secretive smile that reminded me of Kyle. She stepped back, as if to give the knife to me.

Then she darted behind me, pulled me close, and pressed the steel blade to my throat.

↬ *Chapter 15* ↫

I didn't move. I barely dared breathe. "Mom?" I reached for her knife hand, and she pressed her blade against my throat, biting skin.

"*Tara,*" I whispered. "*Go away.*"

Mom drew the knife back. I heard her take one step away, then a second, and a third. My neck stung where the blade had been.

There was a blur of motion—I whirled to see Karin knock the knife from Mom's hand and sweep her feet out from under her. How had she moved so fast? Mom fell into the mud. I drew my own knife and lunged at the Lady.

She stepped lightly away from my blade, toward Karin. I stumbled and spun around.

"I do believe that was a direct challenge to my magic

and my power." The Lady's voice was soft as silk, sharp as steel. She smiled as her fingers closed around Karin's wrist. "And so you forfeit the protections of kinship and rank."

Karin slipped from her hold—too late. She began to *change,* arms stretching into branches, feet rooting down into the earth.

"Karin!" I couldn't let winter take her, too. *"Karinna, come here!"* My magic rolled harmlessly away, and I felt the Lady's stronger magic rushing over her daughter, consuming her as fire consumed wood.

"I deny you, Arianna." Bark flowed over Karin's chest and neck, through her hair. "I deny you, and your games, and every last claim you have on me." The last words came out with a gasp as her eyes and mouth disappeared within the thick bark of a winter oak. A spark of life reached for me from within that tree, then pulled abruptly back.

"Indeed." The Lady looked to the silver moon. "It is poorly played, Karinna."

I lunged at the Lady again. Again she stepped away, so quickly I wasn't sure how I'd missed her. Matthew snarled and moved to her side. Mom grabbed her knife with her left hand, stood, and stumbled toward me. Her right hand hung limp at the wrist—Karin had done something to it when she'd knocked the knife away.

Elin fluttered from the quia tree to one of the oak's branches. Mom and I circled each other, both trying for the higher ground, while Kyle sang on behind the quia tree, as if unaware of any of us. I couldn't let Mom strike out with that blade, but I also couldn't hurt her.

I could do whatever I had to, to see the Lady—*Arianna*—stopped. The knowledge settled, cold and hard, inside me. Karin couldn't help now, but she had left me a weapon. It was up to me to use it. I couldn't let the Lady destroy any more human towns.

I sheathed my knife with my right hand. As Mom's eyes followed the movement, I grabbed her wrist with my left, bending it down and away. If I could get the knife from Mom, I still had a chance of protecting her.

She fought me. "I need the knife."

"Why do you need it, Mom?"

"To cut out your heart." She spoke as if it were the most reasonable thing in the world. A smile twitched the Lady's lips as she petted Matthew's fur.

I unbent Mom's fingers from around the hilt. The knife clattered off a rock, and I grabbed it before Mom could. *"Arianna! Go away!"*

The Lady took a single step away before Matthew growled and jumped at me, pushing me backward into the mud. Mom's knife flew from my hand. I felt the wolf's hot breath on my face as his teeth went for my throat.

I rolled us over, pinning him beneath me. *"Matthew!"* I looked right at him as I tried to call the boy out from the wolf. *"Matthew!"*

He twisted and sank his teeth through my coat. Pain shot through my left shoulder. My hold loosened, and the wolf wriggled out from under me. I leaped to my feet, backing away as I drew my own knife from its sheath. *"Go away, Matthew. Go away!"*

He snarled and stalked toward me. I looked into his gray eyes and saw no one I knew there.

"Matthew." My throat was dry. He'd known his name in Clayburn.

He didn't know it now. I backed uphill, clutching my knife, bracing myself to use it if he leaped again. My shoulder throbbed, but I couldn't let that distract me.

"Go 'way, stupid wolf!" Kyle barreled out from behind the quia tree, fists raised.

Matthew whined as he stopped stalking. *"Go away go away go away!"* Kyle didn't use his name. He didn't have to. Matthew whirled from him and fled into the forest. Mom retrieved Father's knife with her good hand. I gripped my own knife tightly. The Lady watched us all, silent and frowning, fireflies glimmering in her hair.

Tears streaked Kyle's cheeks. "Matthew's never mean."

There was no time to offer comfort—or receive it. "Get out of here, Kyle."

Kyle shook his head. "Help you." He ran at the Lady, grabbing something from his pocket and throwing it at her. Ants—I caught the scent of burning fabric an instant before I saw them crawling over the skirt of her dress. Not carpenter ants, but small red fire ants, glowing with the heat they held. Kyle raced back toward the quia tree.

The Lady brushed at her dress as if the ants were but a passing annoyance, though I smelled burning skin. "Kyle," she said. He froze just an arm's length from the tree. "Come here, Kyle, and I shall tell you just how much I despise animal speakers."

"Okay." Kyle's voice was very small. He turned and walked back toward her.

Something tapped the Lady's shoulder. A shadow. She flinched and turned, but the shadow disappeared into the earth as she reached for it.

Johnny. Stupid, silent Johnny—even the Lady couldn't see him coming. I grabbed Kyle with my free arm. My shoulder screamed with pain. Kyle's eyes focused on mine. "Liza?" He sounded uncertain.

I wanted to give Kyle the leaf again—but I'd have no

chance against the Lady if I did that. "Kyle, you need to run away now. You need to hide."

"Help Johnny now." Kyle fought my hold. "Run later."

"*Kyle.*" I set my hand firmly on his shoulder. *"Run away. Hide. Don't come back until the Lady is gone. Run!"*

"Don't want to—" Kyle flashed me a betrayed look. Then he wrenched free and ran, past the quia and the oak with Elin huddled on its branch. His feet pounded as he disappeared down the far side of the hill.

I turned back to the Lady, my knife still in hand. Johnny was gone—I hoped he'd followed Kyle. I hoped he could protect him, because I couldn't, not anymore.

The Lady brushed at her smoldering skirt, and dozens of tiny gray moths flew away from where the ants had been. Mom moved to her side, holding her knife as well.

"Arianna! Go away!" I put all the power I could into those words. The Lady laughed, as if I were a fool to imagine that my magic could touch her, but again she stepped back. I felt the thread of my magic between us. Was that thread strong enough that I could send her farther away, so far she'd never draw breath again? I'd held back with Father, with Elin. I'd been right to hold back with them—I didn't dare hold back now. I drew a breath,

knowing I didn't act from anger, only need. *"Go away, Arianna. Go away, go away, go away."*

She took a second step back, and a third—and then she stopped. She didn't look anywhere near to dying. *Harder to hurt, harder to heal.* Faerie folk were not as easy to kill as humans.

"I am sure you have found this quite entertaining," the Lady said in her icy voice. "But the game is about to get more interesting. For I begin to find you tedious, Liza, and so I offer you a choice: either let Tara cut out your heart, as I have commanded, or I shall order her to turn the knife on herself instead. I will allow you to decide."

"Go away, Arianna." My voice sounded small and strained. My shoulder hurt so much.

The Lady took one more step away. "Do that again and I shall decide for you—and your mother will die more slowly for your disobedience. Don't you believe you deserve a slow death, Tara, for bringing the humans against us?"

Mom turned her cloudy gaze to Arianna. She nodded and clutched her knife more tightly.

"So you see," the Lady said, "your mother is eager for death, and I am eager to give it to her. Yet still I offer you a choice. Still I allow you to play this game. What say you?"

I didn't know how to play games. I knew only that this

was deadly serious, and that the Lady would have both our lives if she could. I gauged the distance between Mom and me. If I could somehow render Mom unconscious, she wouldn't be able to carry out the Lady's commands. The Lady followed my gaze and raised an eyebrow, and I knew she'd stop me before I could get there—and my injured shoulder would slow me down. I couldn't get at the Lady with my knife, and I couldn't get at her with my magic. I had no other weapons.

I couldn't let her kill Mom the way she'd killed Johnny. If it came down to that, I knew I'd let Mom take my life instead—and what then? What would happen when Mom woke from this nightmare and saw what she'd done?

Before then, the Lady would have the leaf I wore and, with it, Caleb's life. She'd no doubt find Caleb and Karin's town, too, and other towns I didn't know after that. I couldn't let that happen. I needed to play this game after all.

I thought of the offer the Lady had made to Karin. I didn't want to trade away anyone's life—I wasn't sure I had a choice.

"Your decision, Liza."

I sheathed my knife. "I will give up the leaf I wear, if you will give me your word that you will leave the human towns that remain in this world alone."

The Lady lifted her head. A breeze blew, and the fireflies in her hair glowed more brightly. "You *are* an interesting child. Yet you ask much for Kaylen's life. I will leave this town alone, nothing more."

My town's people might die yet if spring didn't come, and Karin hadn't stopped at saving only my town. I fought not to look away from the Lady's bright eyes. Who was I to negotiate with such power?

I was the only one left to do so. I forced my thoughts away from the pain in my shoulder and focused on choosing my words. "You will leave all the human towns, or I will keep the leaf."

Arianna crushed her wineglass into the mud with her boot. "You try my patience, Liza. I will not harm any human who remains within this world's few surviving towns. You will give up the leaf and never seek to hold it again. Are we agreed?"

I looked at my mother. She gave me a bright, empty smile as she twirled the knife in her hand. She'd left me, she'd chosen others over me—but she hadn't wanted to choose, any more than Karin had, any more than I did. She was only human. She was only my mother. The thought filled me with a strange, aching sorrow.

I drew my knife again and flung it away, into the brambles. "We are agreed." Whatever happened next, the human towns would be safe. I reached between my jacket and my sweater to clutch the silver chain.

"You have given your word." The Lady's voice was velvet soft. She held out a pale hand.

The stars glittered, cold and distant, above me. I would protect those *I* could. I would do exactly as I had promised and give up the leaf I wore.

In a single motion I drew the chain from around my neck and draped it over my mother's head.

"Mom," I said, my voice steady, sure now of what I needed to do. "Wake up."

~ *Chapter 16* ~

Mom drew me close, and I knew, in that embrace, that she was my mother once more. I fought the longing to stay there, to believe that she could protect me.

I knew better. I pulled free and ran, sure of what must happen next. I'd kept my word—but that wouldn't save me. I could only hope the Lady was truly bound to keep her word as well, to leave my people alone.

"*Liza!*" There was nothing soft in the Lady's voice now. I fell to my knees at the power there. She was before me in an instant, lifting my chin, forcing me to look into her bright eyes. Fear trembled beneath my skin. That fear was already fading. I knew I would do whatever the Lady asked of me.

Mom circled around behind her, holding her knife.

The Lady held up a hand, not turning. "One more

step, Tara, and I shall order your daughter to pluck out her own eyes. Would you like that, Liza?"

"Yes." My fingers moved toward my face. I wondered what it would be like to feel my nails pierce that soft flesh. Would my blood please the Lady?

Had Johnny's blood pleased her? I felt a ripple of fear at that thought, but it was a distant thing, as distant as the ache in my shoulder.

Mom went very still. "It's me you want. Let Liza go. She is no part of this." I saw fear in her eyes, and anger, and understood neither of them.

"Oh, but she is. The moment you seduced my son into withdrawing his glamour from you and betraying his people, you and all that is yours became very much my concern." Arianna reached for my hands and drew me to my feet. "You are a clever girl, aren't you, Liza?" I frowned, not sure whether being clever was good or not, as the Lady went on. "Yet I can be clever, too. I note that neither you nor your mother are within the borders of your town, and so my promises do not apply to you. All humans leave their towns, for one purpose or another." She glanced at the oak branch from which Elin watched us, utterly silent. "And my granddaughter has made no promises. It will be a small matter for us to destroy your people. The terms of your trade are not as well thought out as you believed."

Her words should have troubled me, but they didn't. Mom looked near to tears, though. I'd always hated to see her cry. "It's okay." I leaned back against the Lady. "There's nothing to be afraid of." *Not anymore.*

The look that crossed Mom's face was a terrible thing. "To think I wanted to bring our children back to your world when they came into their magic," she said. "I thought they'd be safer in your world than mine. I thought surely you had perished in the War, and I imagined that with you gone I might find teachers there."

Arianna stroked my hair. "I think you'd better give me the knife, Tara."

Mom stepped back. "Not unless I have your word you won't give it to Liza."

Arianna laughed at that, laughed and laughed. I wasn't sure what was so funny, but I laughed, too. "I do not need your feeble human weapon to hurt Liza." She smiled down at me. "What shall I turn you into, child? A wolf, perhaps, to replace the one taken from me? Or a cat. I could use a good hunting cat, and Tara tells me you are quite the hunter."

"A cat," I agreed. I'd had a cat once, hadn't I? I liked cats.

The sun touched the horizon, and gold light flashed into my eyes. The Lady gripped my shoulder, hurting me—I didn't mind. I'd never feared pain.

Mom clutched her knife. "Surely there is no need—"

My skin melted beneath the Lady's grasp. Something caught fire within my bones—I screamed as they melted like iron in Jayce's forge, melted into the mold the Lady pressed on them. I fell to all fours, and my scream turned into a cat's growl. Not a small cat, like the cats I'd known. A hunting cat, bigger than a wolf. I paced, tail thrashing, strength coursing through me. The night around me seemed sharper than before, the moon brighter.

I flexed my claws. I needed to sharpen them. The Lady drew her hand away. I stalked toward a tall oak, snarling, and raked my claws against the tree. My shoulder screamed in protest. Some shadow within the wood shifted. A hawk cried and threw itself at me, but the creature's wing failed it, and it sank to the ground.

The Lady sighed, reached down, and brushed her fingers over the hawk's feathers. Silver light washed over the bird, and then Elin huddled, naked, on the ground, one arm drawn to her side. Arianna put her hand to my back, drawing me away from the oak. "There is no need for you to punish Karinna, my cat. As a tree she will die, as all trees must in this dying land, and it will not be without pain."

Elin looked up at the Lady, her eyes wide. Arianna reached out and stroked my fur. I purred at the Lady's touch. Power coursed beneath my skin, but I held it back—I could hold back for her. I wasn't afraid, in this powerful body.

Mom stood just a few steps away, clutching her knife. "Liza. Give me some sign you're still in there."

Of course I was still in here. I was better now, stronger—surely Mom could see that. I opened my jaws in a toothy cat smile.

Elin struggled to her feet and took her grandmother's hand. Wind blew her fine hair over her bare skin.

The Lady smiled. "Kill Tara, Liza." Her whisper scraped the inside of my skin. "Kill her now, my powerful cat."

I leaped, releasing taut muscles, knocking Mom onto her back. The knife fell from her grasp. Pain flared through my shoulder as something tore inside it, but that didn't matter. Only doing as the Lady demanded mattered.

"Liza. You're Liza." Mom's voice was hoarse as she fixed her gaze on me, as if she were trying to call me out of the cat, the same way I'd once called a boy out of a wolf, a girl out of a bird. But my mother was no summoner. I would stay a cat, filled with a cat's power. I snarled and lunged at her throat. She threw her arm up, and my teeth dug through her coat sleeve to pierce flesh. The taste of her blood mingled with the taste of goose down and nylon.

Something stirred inside me at that. I drew back,

memory bubbling to the surface. *To do no harm.* I was Liza, and Liza had spoken words—human words. Something about those words was important. They were a promise; that was it. I couldn't break my promises. Yet it didn't feel like harm, this flexing of strength, this drawing of blood. It felt like what I was made for.

Mom's other arm slammed into me, knocking me aside with startling force. She leaped to her feet and ran. She'd run from me before; I remembered that. The Lady released Elin's hand to step toward me—and fell, a remarkably graceless motion. Her dress had tangled around her legs, and its fabric bound her arms to her sides. *Weaver work.* Arianna struggled to her feet. "Kill Tara, my cat! Kill her!"

The words *hurt* as they clawed through my skin. I whirled and ran after Mom. That I was Liza, that I'd made promises—both were less important than that I was the Lady's cat and needed to please her.

Mom wheeled around a trunk and ran back toward me. I bounded past, unable to slow down fast enough. By the moon's light I saw the glint of steel in Mom's hand once more. She leaped at the Lady in her tangled dress, and Arianna fell back to the ground beneath her. Elin pressed her hand to the Lady's shoulder, holding her down, eyes brimming as the cloth of her grandmother's dress wrapped tighter and tighter around her.

They were hurting the Lady. Why were they hurting her? I leaped at Mom's back.

Arianna's hand tore through a bound sleeve to grab my paw. "You and your mother shall suffer yet," she hissed.

I felt my skin and bones burning, melting, *shifting*. I turned from a cat into a wild dog as the Lady's magic poured through me, from a dog into an eagle, from an eagle into a slithering snake. I roared and howled, shrieked and hissed, as faster and faster I changed. Mom crawled out from underneath me. I struggled to get closer to Arianna and the pain she commanded. Mom tried to pull me away, but I fought her. For an instant I was human once more, kneeling naked in the mud and clinging to the Lady's hand as an icy wind raked my skin, and then I was changing once more, slowly changing to immovable stone. The Lady's gaze met mine, and in her eyes I saw winter unending and the knowledge that spring was nothing more than a story. "All things must end," she whispered, and fell still.

Glamour rolled off me, and all at once my thoughts were my own. I was alone—alone and human and very small—my hand clutching the Lady's. She stared at the sky, her dress wrapped around her, binding her legs, constricting her throat. Mom's knife was plunged through her heart.

She wasn't breathing. The magic she'd poured into me had been her last.

"I'm sorry," Elin whispered to her, kneeling beside us. "But you shouldn't have hurt my mother."

"Nor my daughter, either." Mom's voice was grim. Mud streaked her face, and her arm bled freely through her sleeve.

Horror filled me at what I'd nearly done. I tried to pull away from the Lady, but my left hand was strange and heavy in her grasp. I looked down at our clasped hands.

My hand was gray stone past the wrist, and the Lady's fingers were wrapped around it. Mom crouched beside me and uncurled those dead fingers from mine, one by one.

I drew my hand to my face. My stone fingers were curled halfway into a fist. Matthew's leather hair tie was wrapped around my arm just past the place where stone gave way to skin. My stomach churned, and I had to look away. My hand fell to my side, and its weight sent more pain through my shoulder.

I looked to where the Lady lay. Her eyes were dull as tarnished steel, and I could almost see the gray bones beneath her pale skin. As I watched, the fireflies in her hair flickered out, one by one.

"Liza?" There was a question in Mom's voice.

I couldn't look at her. I stumbled to my feet and turned away, ashamed. The cold mud hurt my bare feet, the cold air my bare skin.

Mom wrapped her arms around me from behind. "Don't you *dare* sacrifice yourself to save me, Liza. Not ever again. Enough of this. It ends here." Her voice was scraped raw.

I hadn't saved her. I'd nearly killed her. I would have torn out her throat without a second thought. I shook like a leaf in the wind. I was so, so cold.

Elin touched the Lady's dress, and fibers flowed away from Arianna to wrap around Elin's own bare skin, brown wool sheathing her chest and legs, leaving the weaver in a sleeveless dress and the Lady in a shroud as thin as gauze from Before. Elin stalked to the oak tree— to Karin—and put one hand to the rough bark. Her other arm hung, bruised and scabbed over, by her side.

She was crying. Karin's clothes were scattered around the tree's base, the silver butterfly's wings trembling among them. In the mud and leaf litter between oak and quia, I saw Kyle's footprints disappearing over the hillside, and Matthew's wolf prints as well. I remembered the dead look in Matthew's eyes. I had to find him.

My pants and sweater and wool underwear lay on the ground. I tried to dress myself against the cold, but I couldn't do it with my dead hand and injured shoulder.

Mom helped me. I avoided her eyes as she used her left hand to ease my undershirt and sweater over my head and held out my underwear and pants for me to step into. Her right wrist hung wrong—it was surely broken—and above it, the arm I'd bitten still bled.

"You should have run." I managed to get my boots buckled myself. "You should have run and kept the leaf safe." *Kept yourself safe.*

"You should have known better than to expect me to." Mom handed me my coat. I stepped away from her to put it on.

A hand snaked around from behind me. I felt a knife at my throat once more as the coat fell from my grasp.

"Call her back, Summoner." Elin's voice had a feral edge. "Do it of your own free will or do it under glamour, it matters not. Waste no more time. Do it."

Mom stepped toward us, and Elin stiffened. She was frightened, I realized, frightened of us small, glamourless humans. Her voice thickened into a syrupy sweetness. "Do it now. Call my mother back."

"Stop!" I said while my thoughts remained my own. "Of course I want to call Karin back. I'd do more than that for her."

"Why would you?" Elin demanded, the glamour gone from her words. "Why should a human care for my people at all?"

"I don't know your people. But I do know your mother." Karin, with her kindness and her teaching. I didn't know who the plant mage had been Before. I only knew who she was now. "You have my word, Elianna. I'll do all I can to save her. But I can't do anything until you take the knife away."

Elin drew back, taking the knife—one of Karin's knives, with a dark stone blade—with her. "I will kill you if she dies. Do not doubt it."

I ignored her and walked to the oak tree. Deep scores ran down the bark, and sap flowed slowly out of them. I'd done that, too. I forced the thought aside as I softened my gaze. I saw Karin's shadow within the tree—head between her knees, hands pressed to the ground. I felt the spark of life that was Karin, fainter and colder now. She was still there. I put my good hand to the rough bark.

The shadow looked up and shook her head—no.

As a tree she will die, as all trees must in this dying land, and it will not be without pain. The Lady's words, but Karin had said as much when we'd found the townsfolk changed.

"What do you wait for?" Elin demanded. The butterfly was in her hair once more, but the wings had ceased their flapping at last.

"I wait because I fear calling will kill her." A loop of

ivy hung from one of the oak's lower branches. Its leaves were already brown, without Karin to keep them awake. One drifted to the ground, and Karin's shadow shrank a little. I thought of the leaves I'd called from the sleeping maple seed, of how quickly they'd withered and died. I thought of the townsfolk in their trees, dying of winter as well. Winter would kill us all in the end, one way or another.

I turned to the quia tree. The shadow that clung to it seemed sharper, more clear than both Karin's shadow and the shadows of the townsfolk. It slept more lightly than the other trees, too, as if tossing in troubled dreams. I felt cold magic stretch between us once more. I hadn't imagined it—this tree knew me. It remembered me.

As I put my hand to the quia's smooth bark, I felt something more—the sense that this tree's shadow didn't end with its roots but reached far deeper, looking to someplace beyond the human world to remember how to grow.

I didn't know if I'd been right or wrong to plant the quia seed and, in doing so, call winter into this world. I only knew that I had. "This is my responsibility."

"Liza," Mom said. "Not everything is your fault."

"I know that." The War wasn't my fault, nor any of the things Mom, Caleb, and Karin had done during it. And maybe spring would still come on its own, just as it had Before, as the trees found the ancient pathways my people said they'd always followed to wake themselves.

But every moment I waited, the chances that there would be enough life left in Karin's tree to call her out grew fainter. Karin said trees died slowly, but I could *see* the shadow in her tree shrinking. I could wait on spring no longer.

"I have to call it back," I said.

∽ *Chapter 17* ∾

"No one can stop the worlds from winding down." So much despair in Elin's voice. She held her hurt arm close. "Grandmother said so, when we came to your world and found it as dead as ours."

"The Lady doesn't know everything," Mom said.

"Careful, human." Elin's bleakness was tinged with disdain.

Mom laughed, a wild sound. "I'm through fearing your people, Elianna. None can do worse to me than your grandmother has already done."

I kept my hand pressed to the quia tree. In the darkness, its shadow seemed more real than its bark and branches.

"Spring has been late before," Mom said.

Would the other trees follow the quia into spring, as

they had followed it into winter? "I don't know how much time the others have. Would you keep me safe and lose them all?"

Mom didn't answer that. She didn't need to. I looked down, ashamed. Wasn't that what I'd wished of her before this all began? That she could have stayed with me, kept me safe instead of protecting others?

"Do what you need to." Mom rubbed at the arm I'd bitten. "I don't know as much about magic as Karinna and Kaylen, but I'll keep watch as best I can."

I swallowed hard. "Thanks, Mom." My breath puffed in front of me. The ground would freeze again soon.

Mom looked at Elin. "Promise you'll not harm my daughter should she fail."

Elin laughed bitterly. "Why should I make any promises to humans?"

"Because Liza won't do this thing unless you do."

I would do this thing no matter what—but I didn't say so. I couldn't lie, but my mother could. "Promise," I said to Elin, "that you won't harm me or Mom or anyone from my town."

Elin stalked to Karin's tree and leaned her head against it. "I do this for you, not them. I do not understand why you care for these humans so. I will never understand it. I will never understand why you did not take me with you when you went away to fight." If Karin heard, she gave no sign. She'd drawn her shadow arms around herself, and her head was bowed once more.

Elin turned back to us. She'd been crying again. "You have my word."

The moon was higher now, but I could still see the pinpricks of stars, like light through old nylon. I rubbed at the leather around my wrist, feeling stone and skin to either side of it. Matthew and Kyle were both out in that darkness. Even now I chose who to save.

I returned my good hand to the quia's trunk, shivering as my skin touched the tree's cold shadow. All this long winter I'd been cold. I wasn't sure I remembered what spring felt like, let alone how to call it.

My dead hand weighed me down. I focused on the quia's shadow and the restlessness that slept within the tree. "*Grow,*" I whispered to it. "*Seek air, seek sun, seek life!*"

The quia's shadow pulled at me, urging me toward the same uneasy sleep in which it already rested. I pressed my feet firmly into the mud and felt again the way the quia's shadow stretched beyond its roots, deep into some other place—into Faerie? Did Karin's world remember the green my world had forgotten? The Lady had said nothing grew there, but perhaps some thin thread of spring remained. "*Wake!*" I called to the shadow's roots—to that place beyond its roots. "*Grow! Seek air, seek sun, seek light!*"

I called again, and again. I couldn't call my mother to me, nor Matthew, either, not always. I couldn't call Johnny back, or the others I'd lost, even before this long winter. But I could do this. I could call spring. *"Grow!"* I saw, somewhere beyond sight, the way the quia's shadow twisted into a dark rope reaching down out of this world. I saw the thinnest thread of green snaking through the darkness, answering my call. I reached for that thread with my magic, pulling it toward me. *"Grow!"*

Something pulled back, something gray and dying that also answered my call and chased after the green. I held to that thin thread, but the harder I held on, the harder the grayness pulled me in turn, urging me deep into the earth, beyond the earth.

Light drained from the world around me, moon and stars fading to dead gray coals. This wasn't Faerie. Even the desolate Realm the War had left behind held more color and life than this.

Yet I'd been here before. I'd called Caleb back from this dead land where nothing grew. I'd thought I'd escaped it and brought him and the quia seed both back with me.

I thought of dead fields and bare trees, of white bone and gray ash. No one could escape such a place, not for good. All things wound down in the end. I was human. I would die. How could I ever have imagined otherwise?

I tried to think of green things, of living things, but green was only a word, and I no longer remembered what it meant. Winter and death pulled on me. I couldn't fight their wordless call. I closed my eyes and let dead branches wrap around me. I wasn't cold anymore. It wasn't such a bad thing after all to see the worlds wind down.

"Quit it, Liza." A boy's voice, from somewhere behind me. Something about that voice made me angry. It had always made me angry.

"Go away." There was no power in my words—in me.

"Nice try." The boy spoke in front of me now. "Too bad I'm through with the whole disappearing act."

I knew him, but I couldn't call up a name. I curled up small among the branches, not caring as thorns dug into my skin.

"And you complain I hide too much? Seriously, Liza, enough of this. Get up."

"I want to sleep." I was warm and I was safe. Why couldn't this nameless boy leave me alone like everyone else? Dimly I remembered that he'd never left me alone when I'd wanted him to.

"Okay, let's try it this way." Didn't he ever give up? "Open your eyes."

"Will you go away if I open my eyes?"

The boy laughed at that, though I couldn't imagine what was so funny. "I'll think about it," he said.

"Fine," I told him. It took a long time—my eyelids were as heavy as if they'd turned to stone, and even once I got them open, I struggled to focus on the boy who stood slouching before me. "Johnny." He was as colorless as everything else in this place, but he looked real, not like a shadow. That wasn't right. "You're dead."

"And you're not. So you're going to get up, and you're going to get yourself back out there."

I drew the branches closer around me. "Can't."

Johnny rolled his eyes. "This is Liza, who went off into the deadly forest all alone and came back alive, who saved her mother even though she wasn't supposed to have any magic? Do you have any idea how tired I am of hearing about how brave you are? The least you could do is live up to it."

I *wasn't* brave, and I hadn't been alone. Someone had been with me on that journey, but I'd forgotten his name as well. My chest hurt. I didn't want to hurt. What was the point of pain when worlds were winding down?

"I know," Johnny said, though I hadn't spoken aloud. "Been a rough week for both of us. Come on." He held out a hand.

He made everything sound so easy—I reached out and took his hand. His fingers were ice; I gasped at the cold that knifed through me. It turned to a painful tingling as dead branches fell away. I tried to burrow back down among them, but Johnny wouldn't let go.

"Sorry, Liza. You don't get to take the easy way out." He smiled sadly. "Only I get to do that. Promise me you'll take care of Kyle?"

Kyle—there was pain behind that name, too. "I promise." The words came easily. I already had promised that, hadn't I?

Something stabbed at my eyes—light? Johnny shrank from it. "Also, tell Matthew it wasn't his fault, okay? He's like you and Tara—he always blames himself. Tell him."

"All right." I was standing. When had I gotten to my feet?

Johnny laughed softly. "So now you have no choice. You have promises to keep out there. And so I get to go. Thanks, Liza."

The light was growing brighter. Suddenly I wanted light, wanted color, more than anything. *"Come here,"* I whispered, and I felt that light pulling on me, as strongly as the gray had. I wanted spring. I needed spring. *"Seek air, seek light, seek life!"*

Light and color flooded me—too much. I staggered and fell to my knees, but I kept my hand pressed against the quia tree. I was surrounded by color: pink sky, orange dawn, a snaking green thread that yearned toward me. I stood and pulled that thread, pulled it with all the magic I had. For a moment I saw Johnny, a shadow once more, watching me. *"Seek rest,"* I told him.

"Already planning on it," Johnny whispered. Then he was gone, and bright leaves were uncurling all around me—on the quia's branches, on sumac and blackberry, on the brown oak nearby. I needed to do something once I woke the oak tree. What was I supposed to do?

"Karin!" I called. *"Karinna, come here!"*

Sunlight spilled like liquid fire over the horizon. It had been night when I'd started this. How long had I been here? I kept pulling on the green, pulling it out of a land beyond both my world and Faerie, a place where nothing grew—the place where all growing began. The thread thickened into a green rope. The rope grew slippery, seeking to escape my magic's hold. For an instant it did escape, and I slid after it, back down into the gray—

Then Karin was pulling the rope alongside me, and her magic wrapped around mine, adding its strength. Leaves exploded to life all around us. Brambles tangled my ankles. I ignored them. Nothing mattered more than holding on to that rope. We pulled harder, Karin and I, pulled the green out of quia and blackberry and sumac, out of trees farther and farther away. I pulled something more out of some of those farther trees, too, something human only I could call.

Each pull drained something from me in turn. Leafy branches circled my waist, my chest, but I didn't stop. We needed the green. We needed light and life and growth. Thorns pierced my skin, drawing blood. Through the branches, a hand grasped mine. "Spring," Karin whispered. There was so much joy—so much light—in that word. "This world will hold a time longer yet."

I looked for Karin, caught a glimpse of green vines flowing up her neck, of thorns reaching for her eyes. "I'm . . . glad," I managed to say. Green leaves sprouted between our fingers, pushing our hands apart. Tendrils wrapped around my ears, flowed over my face. I couldn't see Karin anymore. I could only see green growth all around. I ached with the brightness of it.

"*Enough.*" Karin's voice was fainter. "*Leave be.*" She spoke to the plants now, not me. "*Let blood and bone go. Seek soil, seek water, seek—*"

My ears rang. Very far away, someone called my name. I struggled toward the sound, but the plants were too strong. They dragged me down, and I fell into the green.

S P R I N G

Green light burned against the insides of my eyes, spreading through my arms, my legs, my thoughts. Green things whispered to me, speaking of hunger and soil, of pounding rain and searing sun. Pinpricks of pain raced along my body, thorns being torn away.

"Hang in there, Lizzy. I've got you."

I tried to put a name to the voice, but I couldn't think through the whispers and the light.

"*Wake up, Liza!*" A child's call—it had no power over me. "*No sleeping! Wake up!*" The child began to cry.

Darkness threatened at the edges of the green. I fought it. I wanted light. I wanted spring. A wolf howled. I tried to answer it, but darkness closed in around me, darkness and ice.

"Come here, Liza." A cold voice—the Lady's voice. "The worlds wind down, and no mere human shall escape their fate." I had no choice. I followed her down into the endless dark, knowing that winter took everything in the end.

"Oh, no, you don't, Liza." A girl's voice. Silver light flooded my sight, chasing the dark away. "I tell you and tell you that you can't leave us but you just—don't—listen." The light grew colder with every word, a cleaner cold with nothing of darkness in it. My arms and legs tingled, as if thawing after a walk in the snow. The tingling *hurt*—I bolted upright, fighting it, sending new pain through my shoulder, over my torn and bleeding skin.

"Stay still, Liza! Caleb's with Karin, so I'm on my own, and I don't want to push too hard—" The girl drew a gulping breath.

I knew her then. "Allie?" That made no sense. Why was Caleb's student here?

"Please, Liza," Allie said. She eased me down again. "I know this is hard. Don't make it harder."

"Allie, how—"

"Later," Mom said. I knew her now, too. "There'll be time later." Mom's hand grasped mine—my right hand, because something was wrong with my left—as Allie's light washed over me again. Too cold—I screamed, and for a time I did nothing but scream. After that, I heard someone crying, and I didn't know whether it was Allie or me.

"You're going to be all right, Liza. You know that, don't you?" Allie sounded so tired. "Only you need to rest now. I'm sorry, but you do." The darkness that wrapped around me was warmer now. Gentler. I fought it, but it pulled me under just the same.

*   *   *

I woke to a feather mattress beneath my back and a dull aching pain that filled my whole body. From someplace out of sight, I heard talking.

"You said you could heal her." Elin's voice was bleak.

"And so I have." Caleb's voice, hard and grim. His being here made no more sense than Allie's being here.

"Why should this world be saved," Elin demanded, "while ours falls to dust?" Caleb had no answer for that.

I opened my eyes. Light stung them. Bright afternoon sunlight, shining around the shutters of Kate's bedroom window. From a chair at my side, Mom reached for my hand. Her face was covered in scratches, her arm bandaged, her wrist in a splint. "You're hurt," I said. Why was she hurt? The plants hadn't attacked her.

They had attacked me. Memory returned slowly, in tattered bits and pieces. Karin and I had called the plants back into the world, but then they'd attacked, because that was what plants did when they were awake.

In a chair at the foot of the bed, Allie jerked awake, and she hurried to my other side. Mom released my hand.

"Allie, what are you doing here?" Allie had followed me before, but that had been long ago, before winter.

Her red hair was tangled, and her eyes were shadowed,

but she gave me a lopsided smile. "Taking care of you, of course. I'm your healer, remember?"

Caleb stepped into the room, his clear hair falling to his shoulders, a coin from Before hanging from a chain over his sweater. He looked no older than Karin. His silver eyes were sunken with weariness, but he smiled when he saw me. "Liza. It is good to see you awake." He and Mom exchanged unreadable looks, and I thought of how he'd held Mom under glamour, how Mom had fled when he'd let the glamour go—but when he moved to Allie's side, I also saw the healer who'd saved Mom's life. Mom's hand brushed the leaf she wore, as if for reassurance.

Allie drew the blankets back. I wore a loose night-shirt. A green plastic frog, a yellow duck, and a pink pig were all tucked in beside me. Scar tissue peeked out from beneath the shirt, and I felt more scratches, itchy and half-healed, rubbing against the wool. I reached for them.

My hand wouldn't listen. Something was wrong—it was too heavy, too stiff. "Oh." I lifted my arm toward me and stared at the gray stone where my hand had been. My stone fingers were half-curled, as if they still clutched the Lady's hand. My hand itched, somewhere deep inside, but when I touched it, I felt nothing. I couldn't hold a bow with such a hand. I couldn't hunt.

Allie bit her lip. "I'm sorry, Liza. There's nothing there to heal. It's stone, but it's perfectly healthy stone. Maybe one day you can find another changer to fix it, but I can't. I tried."

I traced the stone where it softened into skin just above my wrist. I would get used to this. I had no choice.

I shouldn't even be here. "The plants killed me." I'd fallen into their green embrace.

Allie laughed then. "No," she said. "They didn't."

"Karinna's command stopped the plants in time," Caleb said soberly. "Or stopped them enough that Tara and Elianna could pull you free." He reached out and ran his hands over my body, not quite touching me, sending a shiver over my skin just the same.

"It is well," Caleb said. "You're going to be sore for a long while, Liza, but Allison has healed the worst of the damage the newborn plants did to you, as well as the deeper hurts that came from touching the winter sleep that held them."

Allie let out a breath and clutched the edge of the bed. "Told you you were going to be all right." She was shaking, as if she hadn't been as sure as she'd sounded.

Mom held my good hand tightly. "You're hurt, too," I told her.

"I'm fine," she said. "Not all the plants stopped at Karinna's command, that's all. Some of them fought

Elianna and me when we wanted the two of you back. They lost. Kaylen can heal me later, once he's had time to recover."

I glanced at her splinted wrist, her bandaged arm. Not all Mom's injuries had come from the plants. More memories slid into place. Karin had broken her wrist, but her arm—I rolled away, unwilling to face her.

"Don't you dare." Mom reached out and brushed my hair back from my face. "I will not let you blame yourself, Liza. Not for this."

I focused on the stone where my hand should have been. "You don't—"

"I do understand." The steel in Mom's voice surprised me. She'd put a knife through the Lady's heart—I shouldn't have been surprised. "If anyone understands the effects of glamour, it's me."

Allie tugged on Caleb's arm. "What's glamour?" she asked. Caleb looked down, as if ashamed, and didn't answer.

Mom rubbed my back. "I do not blame you," she said firmly. "I will never blame you. I know what it's like."

I knew what it was like now. I knew why Mom had been so frightened when I'd used my magic on her.

"Look at me, Liza."

I'd once gone through fire and glass to save my mother, but just then, nothing was as hard as turning back to her. "You have my word," I said, speaking the promise she'd wanted before I'd left. "I will not use my magic to compel you ever again, not without your consent."

I sat up. Mom drew a shuddering breath and pulled me close. "I had no right to ask that of you," she said.

"You had every right." And I would keep my word, even were magic not compelling me.

When Mom drew away, Allie pressed a cup to my lips. The thin meat broth within soothed my parched throat and calmed my stomach. When I was done, I stood on unsteady feet. My stone hand made my balance strange. I let Allie tie a strip of old sheet into a sling to rest my arm in. The pain in my shoulder was gone.

I moved to the window and pushed the shutters open one-handed. Green flooded my sight. The window faced the forest, and beyond the town the trees were in full leaf, so bright and deep they made the gray sky above seem green as well. A cold breeze blew in, and it smelled of wet growing things. I inhaled deeply. Our crops would grow now. I knew it down to my bones.

Allie hovered by my side. How had she and Caleb known to come? "The trees," I said. "The townsfolk—"

"They're fine," Mom said as I turned back to her. "When you called spring, you called them free from the trees, too. Or maybe they would have changed back anyway once spring came—there's a lot I don't know about magic." Her fingers brushed Caleb's. Forgiving someone for the things they'd done under glamour was one thing, but forgiving them for the glamour itself—I still didn't understand it.

"Ethan's holding on, too," Mom said. "It'll be touch and go for a while, but turning him into a tree was probably the best thing anyone could have done for him. It slowed his dying enough for Kaylen to tend him, though Kaylen only had power enough left to stabilize him, for now. He'll do more later." Mom shook her head. "I wonder what the Lady would think, knowing she'd saved a human life."

I rubbed my arm in its sling. Just thinking about the Lady made me feel cold.

I heard more talking down the hall, from Matthew's room—but it wasn't Matthew I heard. Kyle had sent Matthew away, beyond the Lady's grasp. Why, then, was I suddenly afraid?

I focused on the voices, pushing the fear aside. "I need to return soon." Karin sounded terribly weary. "The Wall will be waking, and the plant speaker I've left behind is largely untrained."

"I don't understand," Elin said. "You risk everything for them."

"Then you shall have to settle for simply accepting

it." Karin's footsteps moved down the hall. Caleb hurried out the door. His steps made no sound—faerie folk never made any sound. Something was wrong. I stumbled as I crossed the room. Mom steadied me as Caleb led Karin inside.

Her eyes were bandaged. "Liza? Give me some sign that you are well, for though Kaylen could not tell me so if it weren't true, I would know for myself."

I remembered thorns reaching for her eyes. "Are you—"

Karin moved toward my voice, and I heard the slight hesitation in her steps. "They may yet heal."

I hadn't thought I'd made any sound, but I must have, for Karin said softly, "It is all right, Liza. The trees are no longer silent. I hear them all around us, speaking of spring, of rain, of turning their leaves toward the sun. You have done more than I dared hope for, and it is an honor to be your teacher."

I glanced at Caleb. Surely he could heal this. He could heal so much.

"Injuries involving connections between body and mind are never wholly under the healer's control." Caleb's voice held steady, as if he were delivering a lesson. "I can only repair the pathways the plants damaged. I cannot make the mind decide to follow where they lead. That will happen or not, over time."

"It is all right," Karin said again, with a faint note of impatience that made me think she'd told Caleb as much before. "We did what needed doing, and in the end the cost was less than I was willing to pay." Karin reached for me. Her hand was crossed with thick pink scars. I took it, and she squeezed my fingers in her own. I'd have given my life to bring back spring, and I knew she'd have done the same. It didn't need saying. We made the decisions we needed to make, paid the prices we had to pay to save what we could.

"You give up much for our people." Mom's words had a strange edge.

Karin lifted her head toward her. "That surprises you?"

Mom looked away to smooth the blankets one-handed. "I have grown accustomed to being surprised, since the War."

"You were wrong, Tara, when you said I would enjoy watching your people die." Karin brushed a hand over the wool nightgown she wore, as if the fabric were strange to her. I saw the outlines of more bandages through the coarse cloth. "I did not enjoy it. I still wake to the memory of their screams. Does that please you?"

Nightmares, I thought. There were worse nightmares than mine.

"No. It doesn't." Mom set the toy frog, duck, and pig atop the blankets. "I'm sorry, Karinna."

I heard an indrawn breath from the doorway. Elin stood there, her arm bandaged as well, the silver butterfly back in her hair. "They cried out when I killed them, too," the girl whispered. "Humans do not die as quietly as our people do."

"No. They do not." Karin released my hand to turn to her daughter. "And were you glad, when they died?"

The sleeves of Elin's brown dress were ragged with tiny knots, as if she'd been worrying them. "No. I thought it necessary, but I was not glad."

Karin stepped toward her daughter. "Later," she said softly, "we will talk."

With a sound that might have been a sob, Elin turned away. She fled down the hall, her steps making no sound against the hardwood floor. Karin sighed, rested her head against her hands, and didn't try to follow.

Outside, rain began pattering gently against the roof. Other footsteps barreled up the stairs, not silent at all. "Liza!" Kyle threw himself at me, wrapping his arms around my legs. "Not sleeping!"

Hope ran in after him, flashing me an apologetic look. "Sorry, Liza. We tried to keep him out so you could rest." The acorns were gone from her hair, and her usual mischievous grin was missing as well. She'd been subject to glamour, too, at least for a short while. *Long enough to be turned into a tree.* There was no one in my town magic hadn't touched now. "Though keeping the other Afters out has been almost as hard," Hope said. "You've no idea how good it is to see you're all right, Liza. We've all been worried. I hear it's thanks to you we don't still have roots and branches, by the way." She laughed uneasily. "We'll make sure the Befores all know that it's you who saved us. They need our magic, whether they like it or not."

I held Kyle close with my good hand. Seeing him was reminder enough I hadn't saved everyone. I looked at Mom. "You know about . . ."

Mom squeezed the plastic pig. "I saw Johnny's shadow. Kyle told me the rest." She looked across the room to Hope. "Brianna?"

Hope muttered a few rude words. "She won't talk to any of us. Told Jayce she's through with magic and won't have it in her house any longer."

Kyle quivered against me. I wouldn't *let* him go back to Brianna, even were she willing to have him. *My responsibility.* "He'll stay with me." I'd promised to take care of him, and one way or another I would.

Kyle stopped shaking and looked up, his eyes wide.

Mom set the plastic pig back on the bed, picked up the frog. "Liza. You can't do everything. Especially when, if I understand properly, Karinna is to teach you now. You'll be leaving, for a time at least, whether I want it or not, won't you?"

I pressed my lips together. "I'll figure it out. This needs doing, too."

"I didn't say it didn't. You're good at many things, Liza, but has it occurred to you that maybe you don't know much about how to raise a child?" I opened my mouth to protest, but Mom went on. "And has it also occurred to you that if Kyle is going to live with you, he'll be living with me, too? Charlotte and her father are working on the house. We'll be able to go home soon." Mom handed me the frog and reached down to wipe a smudge of dirt from Kyle's cheek. "We'll do this together, Liza. He'll stay with *us*."

"Stay with you?" The strained hope in Kyle's voice made my chest hurt.

I let out a breath, surprised at the weight Mom's words lifted. I handed Kyle the frog. "You'll stay with us. Me and Mom."

"I like Tara," Kyle agreed. He solemnly tucked the frog into his pocket.

Hope nodded. "We'll all help, too. Afters stick together. I'll tell the others." She slipped out of the room and down the stairs.

Kyle smiled slyly and drew something out of his pocket for me in turn. A small plastic dinosaur.

"Oh, Kyle, how did you—" I thought of Ethan and Ben, of that walk with Matthew through the forest not so long ago.

"Matthew." I squeezed the dinosaur so hard my hand ached. "Where is he?"

"Hurt," Kyle whispered. "Outside."

The last of my thoughts came clear. When I'd seen Matthew, he hadn't known his name. *A wolf running, his shadow dissolving behind him.* I shivered in my thin nightshirt. In the vision he'd been lost beyond all calling back.

But that was—had been—the future. It might not have happened yet. I headed for Kate's dresser, searching for clothes.

Allie grabbed my good arm. "Liza, you need rest—"

I pulled away and removed my sling. I managed to get a pair of Kate's pants on one-handed and dug through a drawer for some socks.

"He's all right," Mom said quietly. "As far as any of us can tell, he's just frightened and not ready to change back. He ran all the way to Caleb's town and back. That would take a lot out of anyone."

He hadn't known his name, but he'd known to run for help. Or maybe he'd just remembered the journey he'd started what seemed so long ago, to bring Caleb to our town, and the promise he'd made then was what had set him back on the path. "Matthew's in trouble." My visions had been clear about that much.

"It can wait," Mom said, though she didn't sound happy about it.

"If Liza's visions speak true, it may not be able to wait." Karin walked around the bed toward me, one hand guiding her along the frame. "And her summoning may be some help. I will go with you, Liza. We will do what we can."

Caleb frowned at that. So did Allie. "You're *terrible* patients," she said.

Karin laughed. "Knowing us both, did you expect otherwise?"

Allie helped me pull a sweater on over my nightshirt while Kyle lined all the plastic animals up on the dresser in front of me. Somewhere among the blankets he'd found Matthew's hair tie, and he set that in front of the toys, like a path for them to follow. Caleb searched the drawers, digging out more clothes for Karin.

As I stepped into my boots, I remembered something else I ought not have forgotten. "Caleb, you have to see to Mom, too. Not just because of her wrist. She's ill again, though she won't admit it."

"No, she isn't." Allie sounded puzzled. I looked to Caleb. Maybe Allie couldn't see it, but surely Caleb could. He'd healed Mom before.

Caleb seemed very interested in staring at his own feet. So did Mom.

"Oh my goodness." Allie burst out laughing as she buckled my boot. "You haven't told her, have you?" Karin lifted her head as she pulled on a sweater, and I knew that whatever Allie meant, Karin didn't know about it, either.

"Told me *what*?"

Allie kept laughing. "No one's sick, Liza. The baby-to-be is as healthy as any baby can be this early on, and your mom's healthy, too."

"*What?*" I got to my feet, my other boot still unbuckled. Questions I didn't have time for flooded me. Why hadn't Mom told me this, either? How could she let me worry? I seized on the least important—the safest—question. "It's been six months since your last visit," I told Caleb severely. If Mom was six months pregnant, we all would have known.

"Baby?" Kyle asked, as if he'd only just heard.

"There have been . . . other visits," Caleb said gravely. I hadn't known that faerie folk could blush until then.

"To check for any lingering effects of the radiation." Mom was blushing, too, even as she took Caleb's hands in her own. "I'm sorry, Lizzy. I wasn't sure myself at first, and then I wasn't sure how to tell you. It didn't seem possible, honestly."

"That's because it isn't supposed to be possible." Karin quietly pulled on pants and wool socks. "Or so we were taught. I am glad, for once, to be wrong."

"Truly?" Mom asked her.

"Truly," Karin said.

I felt more questions welling up. Another sister or brother—a *half* sister or brother—I couldn't think about this now. It could wait, and Matthew couldn't. I bolted for the stairs, not waiting for Karin to find shoes so she could follow. Allie ran after me, and Kyle, too. At the bottom of the staircase, Allie stopped me long enough to buckle my other boot. I'd forgotten my sling, and my balance was off again, but I didn't go back. In the living room I caught a glint of light. Kate's mirror—someone had drawn the wall hanging back from it. The light grew brighter, and in that light I saw—

Elin, putting her hand to the silvered glass. "I'm sorry, but I cannot stay here with you—with them." Elin's eyes were puffy with tears, but her gaze held steady. She took the butterfly from her hair and set it down. "I'm going home. Someone has to look after what remains of our people, too." She stepped through the glass. I caught a glimpse of blackened trees beneath a hot blue sky, and then Elin was gone.

Her silver butterfly lay on the floor beside the mirror. A message, but not for me. There'd be time to worry about that later, too. I left it there and headed out the door.

Cold rain fell on my hair and my sweater. I held my left arm close and looked at Kyle. "Can you take me to Matthew?"

Kyle nodded and took my good hand, pulling me along. Allie followed right behind. The world around us was so green—I stumbled beneath the weight of it. Townsfolk were outside their houses, pulling up new weeds, because of course I'd called the weeds back with everything else. You didn't get to choose what you called when you pulled life into the world.

In Kate's backyard I saw the shed where Ethan must still be healing, its ruined roof covered with a blue tarp. Seth stood guard outside. Perhaps some of the townsfolk would be grateful that magic had healed them, but others would be more uneasy about strangers than ever.

Kyle led me on, past the Store and into the forest. Around us, oaks and maples moaned as they stretched new leaves toward the rain. A length of bright ragweed crept toward our feet. *"Go away,"* I whispered, and it drew back, more quickly than it would have last spring. Perhaps the plants had grown a little tamer while they'd slept.

We found Matthew hunkered down in a clearing among the trees, his fur soaked and tangled, his belly pressed into the mud. Kate knelt a few paces away, making soothing sounds, but Matthew didn't seem to hear his grandmother.

I knew this place. It looked different without the snow and with the green, but it was the same place we'd found Ethan.

"Matthew wore his paws raw running to our town," Allie whispered. "He made it clear he wanted Caleb and me, but he wouldn't let us get close, and he wouldn't shift back. He was so wild—I don't think he wants to change, Liza."

I walked slowly toward him. "Matthew?"

He whined and buried his nose in his scabbed and bleeding paws. It was Kate who looked up with a tired smile. "It's good to see you awake, Liza."

"I'll bring him home," I told her as I kept walking, ignoring the rain soaking through my clothes. "Just like I promised."

The wolf growled low in his throat. I stopped and held out my hands, stone and flesh. The wolf bared his teeth. His gray eyes were dull, reminding me of a land without color or life. Yet even in that dead land there was green to be found if you were willing to fight for it.

"Call him?" Kyle asked.

"No." I didn't know what would happen if we forced magic on Matthew now. He'd been under glamour far longer than I had. I searched his wolf's eyes for some sign of the boy I knew. It wasn't just that he didn't know me—I didn't know *him,* though the dark markings around his muzzle and eyes were the same as always. He could have been any feral dog. Matthew wasn't there.

"Hurt *inside,*" Kyle whispered. I thought of my vision: Matthew's shadow dissolving behind him as he ran. *All things that live and grow have shadows.* I crouched in the mud, rested my stone hand on my knees, and softened my gaze.

Matthew's shadow wasn't gone. It was dark and clear, a wolf's shadow that fit beneath his fur, tight as skin. "Matthew?" The wolf didn't answer to the name.

I softened my gaze further, eyes aching as I let all focus go. I thought not of the wolf I saw, but of the boy I knew, the one who walked by my side through dark forests. A second shadow came clear, a fainter, human shadow, huddling within the wolf's shadow the way Karin's shadow had huddled within the oak tree.

"Matthew." I looked at the human shadow as I spoke, but I put no command into the words. "Matthew, look at me. Please."

Slowly the shadow looked up. The hunch of his shoulders reminded me not of the boy I knew now, but of the younger child who'd stood, bruised and bloodied, at the edge of our town after changing to a wolf and back again for the first time. "It's all right to be frightened," I said, and only afterward remembered that Karin had spoken the same words to me. I reached out my hand. Matthew's shadow reached out his. Our fingers touched—

Too cold; I jerked back. Matthew's shadow burned colder than the human shadows I'd laid to rest on our forest patrols, colder even than Johnny's shadow. It burned with the cold of winter unending, of the Lady's gaze as she said worlds were winding down.

I had to try again. I had to touch him to have a chance of drawing him out. I became aware of people watching me—not only Allie and Kyle and Kate, but Mom and Caleb with Karin, and others as well. Keeping my gaze on the human shadow within the wolf, I drew a deep breath, then reached out with my other hand, the one made of stone.

The shadow drew back. "I watched," he whispered.

"It wasn't your fault." The shadow shook his head, denying my words. Helping the Lady hurt others was probably the stuff of *his* nightmares. "It's over," I told him.

The wolf remained pressed to the ground, but the human shadow's shoulders shook. "I watched him die."

"I know, Matthew." I didn't deny that pain. I just kept holding out my hand.

Matthew's shadow fingers wrapped around my stone

ones. I stood, and the shadow stood with me. We faced each other, both of us trembling, both of us afraid. The wolf whined, and I saw Matthew looking out through those gray eyes. I reached down with my other hand, and he pressed his muddy nose into it. "Matthew. You're Matthew."

The wolf and his human shadow both bowed their heads, as if that truth were a heavy burden. There was a flash of silver light, and then a human boy stood before me, bare skin streaked with mud, pale hair wet and dripping, human fingers still wrapped around my stone ones. He stumbled forward, falling to his knees. I knelt and gathered him into my arms. His skin was so cold. I rubbed my good hand over his back, trying to warm him. He was here. He was Matthew. I hadn't lost him. The world was not winding down after all.

Caleb whispered something I couldn't quite hear. "Well done," Karin said softly.

"The things I did," Matthew said. "I could have killed Tara. I could have killed *you.*"

"But you didn't." I'd nearly lost him instead—but that hadn't happened, either.

"I brought Johnny back to her. He wouldn't have died if not for me."

"You didn't kill him. She did." In the end he'd been a weapon in the Lady's hands, just like I had.

"He's still dead." So harsh, Matthew's voice. "Nothing can make that right."

I stroked Matthew's hair, which was as wet and muddy as his fur had been. His hands and feet bled. "I'm sorry," I whispered. "I'm sorry I couldn't keep you safe."

"Nothing's safe." Matthew shook in my arms. Someone—Hope—handed me a blanket; I wrapped it around him. Half the town seemed to be watching us.

"You saved me," I told Matthew, "and Karin and Ethan, too." That had to count for something. "You brought Caleb and Allie back in time."

Matthew nodded as if that knowledge, too, were difficult to bear. His shaking eased. "Liza." He took my strange stone hand and cradled it in both his human ones, as if it were terribly precious. I was suddenly aware of how close we were, of his bare skin under the thin blanket. I looked at him. He looked at me. I realized we were both trembling again, and I had an urge to laugh that made no sense at all.

I didn't know which of us moved first, but all at once our lips were pressed together, and my hand was back in his hair, and we were holding each other close as we knelt in the mud. He tasted of earth and wolf and boy and *Matthew*, and I didn't want to ever let him go.

The rain fell harder. Under her breath Hope muttered, "About time."

"Help?" Kyle whispered.

"No," Allie said. "I don't think you can help with this."

I ignored them all. Matthew and I held each other so closely, so fiercely, as if all this world depended on it, and Faerie as well.

We didn't stop until the soil beneath us stirred. We scrambled to our feet then, remembering that we were in a forest, with all the dangers forests held. A bright purple flower unfurled in the brown mud. Matthew and I stepped back as the crocus hissed with the acid it held.

"It's spring," Matthew said, but not as if he believed it.

I looked at the bright trees, at the small spitting flower at our feet, at Matthew's muddy hands holding both of mine. For now I would have to believe for us both.

"I know it is," I said.

❦ Acknowledgments ❧

Many thanks to: C. S. Adler, Dawn Dixon, Larry Hammer, Jill Knowles, Patricia McCord, and Jennifer J. Stewart for reading the manuscript, often on short notice. Everyone at Kindling Words West 2009 and 2010 for their positive energy and regular reminders that I knew how to tell this story. Petra Brun for loaning me her daughter Elín's name. Rick Holderman for answering my hawk questions. My editor, Jim Thomas, without whom this would be a far weaker book. Chelsea Eberly, Ellice M. Lee, Meg O'Brien, and everyone at Random House who saw the story out into the world. My agent, Nancy Gallt, without whom Liza's journey might never have begun, and her assistant, Marietta Zacker. And especially, my thanks to all the readers who asked to see more of Liza and her world and who encouraged me to return there.

Janni Lee Simner lives in the Arizona desert, where she has traded winters with snowfalls and gray trees for winters with rainfalls and green trees. *Faerie Winter* is the sequel to her first young adult novel, *Bones of Faerie*. Janni is also the author of the young adult fantasy *Thief Eyes*, as well as four books for younger readers and more than thirty short stories, including one in the urban fantasy anthology *Welcome to Bordertown*.

To learn more about Janni, visit her website at simner.com.